BARK

Lorrie Moore has received numerous grants and awards for her work, including the O. Henry Award and the *Irish Times* Prize for Literature. Her most recent novel, *A Gate at the Stairs*, was shortlisted for both the PEN/Faulkner Award for Fiction and the Orange Prize for Fiction in 2010.

by the same author

A GATE AT THE STAIRS
BIRDS OF AMERICA
WHO WILL RUN THE FROG HOSPITAL?
LIKE LIFE
ANAGRAMS
SELF-HELP

LORRIE MOORE

BARK

Stories

FABER & FABER

First published in the United States in 2014 by Alfred A. Knopf,
a division of Random House LLC, New York

First published in the UK in 2014 by Faber & Faber
Bloomsbury House
74–77 Great Russell Street
London WCIB 3DA
This export edition first published in 2014

Printed and bound by CPI Group (UK) Ltd, Croydon, CRO 4YY

The right of Lorrie Moore to be identified as author
of this work has been asserted in accordance with Section 77 of the
Copyright, Designs and Patents Act 1988

Selected stories in this collection first appeared in the following:
"Foes" (2008) in *The Guardian;* "Subject to Search" (2013) in *Harper's;*
"Debarking" (2003), "The Juniper Tree" (2005), "Paper Losses" (2006), and
"Referential" (2012) in *The New Yorker;* and "Wings" (2012) in *The Paris Review.*

Grateful acknowledgment is made to HarperCollins Publishers for permission to
reprint an excerpt from "Vita Nova" from *Vita Nova* by Louise Glück. Reprinted
by permission of HarperCollins Publishers.

*This is a work of fiction. Names, characters, places, and incidents
either are the product of the author's imagination or are used fictitiously.
Any resemblance to actual persons, living or dead, events,
or locales is entirely coincidental.*

A CIP record for this book
is available from the British Library

ISBN 978–0–571–27391–1

2 4 6 8 10 9 7 5 3 1

for Deborah Rogers and Deborah Treisma

I shall still be here . . . growing my bark
around the wire fence like a grin.

Caroline Squire, "An Apple Tree Spouts
Philosophy in an Office Car Park"

In the splitting up dream
we were fighting over who would keep
the dog,
Blizzard. You tell me
what that name means. He was
a cross between
something big and fluffy
and a dachshund. Does this have to be
the male and female
genitalia? Poor Blizzard,
why was he a dog? He barely touched
the hummus in his dogfood dish.

Louise Glück, from "Vita Nova"

Don't be gruff. Anything that falls on the floor is
mine.

Amy Gerstler, "Interview with a Dog"

Contents

DEBARKING

Ira had been divorced six months and still couldn't get his wedding ring off. His finger had swelled doughily around it— a combination of frustrated desire, unmitigated remorse, and misdirected ambition, he said to friends. "I'm going to have to have my entire finger surgically removed." The ring (supposedly gold, though now that everything he had ever received from Marilyn had been thrown into doubt, who knew) cinched the blousy fat of his finger, which had grown around it like a fucking happy vine. "Maybe I should cut off the whole hand. And send it to her," he said on the phone to his friend Mike, with whom he worked at the State Historical Society. "She'll understand the reference." Ira had already ceremoniously set fire to his wedding tux—hanging it on a tall stick in his backyard, scarecrow-style, and igniting it with a Bic lighter. "That sucker went up really fast," he gasped apologetically to the fire marshal, after the hedge caught too, and before he was brought overnight to the local lockdown facility. "*So* fast. Maybe it was, I don't know, like the residual dry-cleaning fluid."

"You'll remove that ring when you're ready," Mike said now. Mike's job approving historical preservation projects on old houses left him time to take a lot of lenient parenting courses and to read all the lenient parenting books. "Here's what you do for your depression. I'm not going to say lose yourself in charity work. I'm not going to say get some perspective by

3

watching our country's news each evening and by contemplating those worse off than yourself, those, say, who are about to be blown apart by bombs. I'm going to say this: Stop drinking, stop smoking. Eliminate coffee, sugar, dairy products. Do this for three days, then start everything back up again. *Bam.* I guarantee you, you will be so happy."

"I'm afraid," Ira said softly, "that the only thing that would make me happy right now is snipping the brake cables on Marilyn's car."

"Spring," Mike said helplessly, though it was still only the end of winter. "It can really hang you up the most."

"Hey. You should write songs. Just not too often." Ira looked at his hands. Actually he *had* once gotten the ring off in a hot, soapy bath, but the sight of his denuded finger, naked as a child's, had terrified him and he had shoved the ring back on.

On the other end of the phone Ira could hear Mike sighing and casting about. Cupboard doors closed loudly. The refrigerator puckered open, then *whooshed* shut. Ira knew that Mike and Kate had had their troubles—as the phrase went—but always their marriage had held. "I'd divorce Kate," Mike had once confided to Ira, "but she'd kill me." "Look," Mike said now, "why don't you come to our house Sunday for a little Lent dinner. We're having some people by and who knows?"

"Who knows?" asked Ira.

"Yes—who knows?"

"What's a Lent dinner?"

"We made it up. For Lent. We didn't really want to do Mardi Gras. Too disrespectful, given the international situation."

"So you're doing Lent. I'm unclear on Lent. I mean, I know what Lent means to those of us in the Jewish faith. But we don't usually commemorate these transactions with meals. Usually there's just a lot of sighing."

"It's like a pre-Easter Prince of Peace dinner," said Mike slowly.

There were no natural predators in this small, oblivious, and tolerant community, and so strange creatures and creations abounded. "Prince of *Peace*? Not—of *Minneapolis*?"

"You're supposed to give things up for Lent. Last year we gave up our faith and reason; this year we are giving up our democratic voice, our hope." Ira had already met most of Mike's *goyishe* friends. Mike himself was low-key, tolerant, self-deprecating to a flaw. A self-described "ethnic Catholic," he once complained dejectedly about not having been cute enough to have been molested by a priest. "They would just shake my hand very quickly," he said. Mike's friends, however, tended to be tense, intellectually earnest Protestants who drove new, metallic-hued cars and who within five minutes of light conversation could be counted on at least twice to use the phrase "strictly within the framework of." "Kate has a divorcée friend she's inviting," Mike said. "I'm not trying to fix you up. I really hate that stuff. I'm just saying come. Eat some food. It's the start of Eastertime and, well, hey: we could use a Jew over here." Mike laughed heartily.

"Yeah, I'll reenact the whole thing for you," said Ira. He looked at his swollen ring finger again. "Yessirree. I'll come over and show you all how it's done."

Ira's new house, though it was in what his realtor referred to as "a lovely, pedestrian neighborhood," abutting the streets named after presidents, boasting, instead, streets named after fishing flies (Caddis, Hendrickson, Gold-Ribbed Hare's Ear Road), was full of slow drains, leaky burners, stopped-up pipes, and excellent dust for scrawling curse words. *Marilyn blows sailors.* The draftiest windows he duct-taped up with sheets of plastic on the inside, as instructed by Homeland Security; cold air billowed the plastic inward like sails on a boat. On a windy day it was quite something. "Your whole house could fly away," said Mike, looking around.

"Not really," said Ira. "But it *is* spinning. It's very interesting, actually."

The yard had already grown muddy with March and the flower beds were greening with the tiniest sprigs of stinkweed and quack grass. By June the chemical weapons of terrorism aimed at the heartland might prove effective in weeding the garden. "This may be the sort of war I could really use!" Ira said out loud to a neighbor. Mike and Kate's house, on the other hand, with its perfect lines and friendly fussiness, reeking, he supposed, of historical preservation tax credits, seemed an impossible dream to him, something plucked from a magazine article about childhood memories conjured on a deathbed. Something seen through the window by the Little Match Girl. Outside, the soffits were perfectly squared. The crocuses were like bells and the Siberian violets like grape candies scattered in the grass. Inside, the smell of warm food almost made him weep, and with his coat still on he rushed past Kate to throw his arms around Mike, kissing him on both cheeks. "All the beautiful men must be kissed!" Ira exclaimed.

After he got his coat off, and had wandered into the dining room, he toasted with the champagne he himself had brought. There were eight guests there, most of whom he knew to *some* degree, but really that was enough. That was enough for every-one. Still, they raised their glasses with him. "To Lent!" Ira cried. "To the final days!" And in case that was too grim, he added, "And to the coming Resurrection! May it happen a little closer to home this time! Jesus Christ!" Soon he wandered back into the kitchen and, as he felt was required of him, shrieked at the pork. Then he began milling around again, apologizing for the Crucifixion: "We really didn't intend it," he murmured, "not really, not the killing part? We just kind of got carried away? You know how spring can get a little crazy, but believe me, we're all really, really sorry." Kate's divorced friend was named Zora, and was a pediatrician. Although no one else did, she howled with laughter, and when her face wasn't blasted apart with it or her jaw snapping mutely open and shut like a scissors (in what Ira recognized was postdivorce hysteria; "How long have you been divorced?" he later asked her. "Eleven years," she replied), Ira could see she was very beautiful: short black hair; eyes a clear, reddish hazel, like orange pekoe tea; a strong aquiline nose, probably a snorer; thick lashes that spiked out wrought and black as the tines of a fireplace fork. Her body was a mix of thin and plump, her skin lined and unlined, in that rounding-the-corner-to-fifty way. *Age and youth,* he chanted silently, *youth and age, sing their songs on the very same stage.* Ira was working on a modest little volume of doggerel, its tentative title *Women from Venus; Men from Penis.* Either that, or *Soccer Dad: The Musical.*

Like everyone he knew, he could discern the hollowness in people's charm only when it was directed at someone other than himself. When it was directed at him, the person just seemed so totally *nice.* And so Zora's laughter, in conjunction with her beauty, doomed him a little, made him grateful beyond reason.

———

Immediately, he sent her a postcard, one of newlyweds drag-ging empty Spam cans from the bumper of their car. He wrote: *Dear Zora, Had such fun meeting you at Mike's.* And then he wrote his phone number. He kept it simple. In courtship he had a history of mistakes, beginning at sixteen with his first girlfriend, for whom he had bought at the local head shop the coolest thing he had then ever seen in his life: a beautifully carved wooden hand with its middle finger sticking up. He himself had coveted it tremulously for a year. How could she not love it? Her contempt for it, and then for him, had left him feeling baffled and betrayed. With Marilyn he had taken the other approach and played hard to get, which had turned their relationship into a never-ending Sadie Hawkins Day, with subsequent marriage to Sadie an inevitably doomed thing— a humiliating and interminable Dutch date.

But this, the Spam postcard and the note, he felt contained the correct mix of offhandedness and intent. This elusive mix—the geometric halfway point between stalker and Rip van Winkle—was important to get right in the world of middle-aged dating, he suspected, though what did he really know of this world? It had been so long, the whole thing seemed a kind of distant civilization, a planet of the apings!—graying, human flotsam with scorched internal landscapes mimicking the young, picking up where they had left off decades ago, if only they could recall where the hell that was. Ira had been a mar-ried man for fifteen years, a father for eight (poor little Bekka, now rudely transported between houses in a speedy, ritualistic manner resembling a hostage drop-off), only to find himself punished for an idle little nothing, nothing, nothing flirtation with a colleague, punished with his wife's *actual* affair and false business trips (Montessori conventions that never existed), and finally a petition for divorce mailed from a motel. Observing others go through them, he used to admire midlife crises, the courage and shamelessness and existential daring of them, but after he'd watched his own wife, a respectable nursery school teacher, produce and star in a full-blown one of her own, he found the sufferers of such crises not only self-indulgent but greedy and demented, and he wished them all weird unnatural deaths with various contraptions easily found in garages.

He received a postcard from Zora in return. It was of Van Gogh's room in Arles. Beneath the clockface of the local postmark her handwriting was big but careful, some curlicuing in the *g*'s and *f*'s. It read, *Had such fun meeting you at Mike's.* Wasn't that precisely, word for word, what he had written to her? There was no *too,* no emphasized *you,* just the exact same words thrown back at him like in some lunatic postal Ping-Pong. Either she was stupid or crazy or he was already being too hard on her. Not being hard on people—"You *bark* at them," Marilyn used to say—was something he was trying to work on. When he pictured Zora's lovely face, it helped his tenuous affections. She had written her phone number and signed off with a swashbuckling *Z*—as in *Zorro.* That was cute, he supposed. He guessed. Who knew. He had to lie down.

He had Bekka for the weekend. She sat in the living room, tuned to Cartoon Network. She liked Road Runner and *Justice League.* Ira would sometimes watch her mesmerized face, the cartoons flashing on the creamy screen of her skin, her eyes still and wide, bright with reflected shapes caught there like holograms in marbles. He felt inadequate as her father, but in general attempted his best: affection, wisdom, reliability, plus not ordering pizza every night, though tonight he had again caved in. Last week Bekka had said to him, "When you and Mommy were married we always had mashed potatoes for supper. Now you're divorced and we always have spaghetti."

"Which do you like better?" he had asked.

"Neither!" she had shouted, summing up her distaste for everything. "I hate them both."

Tonight he had ordered the pizza half plain cheese, and half with banana peppers and jalapeños. The two of them sat together in front of *Justice League*, with TV trays, eating slices from their respective sides. Chesty, narrow-waisted heroes in bright colors battled their enemies with righteous confidence and, of course, laser guns. Bekka finally turned to him. "Mommy says that if her boyfriend Daniel moves in I can have a dog. A dog and a bunny."

"*And* a bunny?" Ira said. When the family was still together, unbroken, the four-year-old Bekka, new to numbers and the passage of time, used to exclaim triumphantly to her friends, "Mommy and Daddy say I can have a dog! When I turn eighteen!" There'd been no talk of bunnies. But perhaps the imminence of Easter had brought this on. He knew Bekka loved animals. She had once, in a bathtime reverie, named her five favorite people, four of whom were dogs. The fifth was her own blue bike.

"A dog *and* a bunny," Bekka repeated, and Ira had to repress images of the dog with the rabbit's bloody head in its mouth.

"So, what do you think about that?" he asked cautiously, wanting to get her opinion on the whole Daniel thing.

Bekka shrugged and chewed. "Whatever," she said, her new word for "You're welcome," "Hello," "Good-bye," and "I'm only eight." "I really just don't want all his stuff there. Already his car blocks our car in the driveway."

"Bummer," said Ira, his new word for "I must remain as neutral as possible" and "Your mother's a whore."

"I don't want a stepfather," Bekka said.

"Maybe he could just live on the steps," Ira said, and Bekka smirked, her mouth full of mozzarella.

"Besides," she said. "I like Larry better. He's stronger."

"Who's Larry?" Ira said, instead of "Bummer."

"He's this other dude," Bekka said. She sometimes referred to her mother as a "dudette." "She's a dudette, all right," Ira would say.

"Bummer," said Ira now. "Big, big bummer."

He phoned Zora four days later, so as not to seem discouragingly eager. He summoned up his most confident acting. "Hi, Zora? This is Ira," and then waited—narcissistically perhaps, but what else was there to say?—for her response.

"Ira?"

"Yes. Ira Milkins."

"I'm sorry," she said. "I don't know who you are."

Ira gripped the phone and looked down at himself, suddenly finding nothing there. He seemed to have vanished from the neck down. "We met last Sunday at Mike and Kate's?" His voice quavered. If he ever actually succeeded in going out with her, he was going to have to take one of those date-rape drugs and just pass out on her couch.

"Ira? Ohhhhhhhhh—Ira. Yeah. The Jewish guy."

"Yeah, the Jew. That was me." Should he hang up now? He did not feel he could go on. But he must go on. *There* was a man of theater for you.

"That was a nice dinner," she said.

"Yes, it was."

"I usually skip Lent completely."

"Me, too," said Ira. "It's just simpler. Who needs the fuss?"

"But sometimes I forget how reassuring and conjoining a meal with friends can be, especially at a time like this."

Ira had to think about the way she'd used *conjoining*. It sounded New Agey and Amish, both.

"But Mike and Kate run that kind of house. It's all warmth and good-heartedness."

Ira thought about this. What other kind of home was there to run, if you were going to bother? Hard, cold, and mean: that had been his own home with Marilyn, at the end. It was like those experimental monkeys with the wire-monkey moms. What did the baby monkeys know? The wire mother was all they had, all they knew in their hearts, and so they clung to it, as had he, even if it was only a coat hanger. *Mom.* So much easier to carve the word into your arm. You were used to pain. You'd been imprinted. As a child, for a fifth-grade science project, in the basement of his house, he'd once tried to reproduce Konrad Lorenz's experiment with baby ducks. But he had screwed up with the incubation lights and had cooked the ducks right in their eggs, stinking up the basement so much that his mother had screamed at him for days. Which was a science lesson of some sort—the emotional limits of the *Homo sapiens* working Jewish mom—but it was soft science, so less impressive.

"What kind of home do *you* run?" he asked.

"Home? Oh, I mean to get to one of those. Right now, actually, I'm talking to you from a pup tent."

Oh, she was a funny one. Perhaps they would laugh and laugh their way into the sunset. "I *love* pup tents," he said. What was a pup tent exactly? He'd forgotten.

"Actually, I have a teenage son, so I have no idea what kind of home I have anymore. Once you have a teenager, everything changes."

Now there was silence. He couldn't imagine Bekka as a teenager. Or rather, he could, sort of, since she often acted like one already, full of rage at the incompetent waitstaff that life had hired to take and bring her order.

"Well, would you like to meet for a drink?" Zora asked finally, as if she had asked it many times before, her tone a mingling of both weariness and the cheery, pseudoprofessionalism of someone in the dully familiar and official position of being single and dating.

"Yes," said Ira. "That's exactly why I called."

"You can't imagine the daily dreariness of routine pediatrics," said Zora, not touching her wine. "Ear infection, ear infection, ear infection. Whoa. Here's an exciting one: juvenile onset diabetes. Day after day you just have to look into the parents' eyes and repeat the same exciting thing: 'There are a lot of viruses going around.' I had thought about going into pediatric oncology, because when I asked other doctors why they'd gone into such a seemingly depressing thing, they said, 'Because the *kids* don't get depressed.' That seemed interesting to me. And hopeful. But then when I asked doctors in the same field why they were retiring early, they said they were sick of seeing kids die. The kids don't get depressed, they just die! These were my choices in med school. As an undergraduate I took a lot of art classes and did sculpture, which I still do a little, to keep those creative juices flowing! But what I would really like to do now is write children's books. I look at some of those books out in the waiting room and I want to throw them in the fish tank. I think, *I could do better than that.* I started one about a hedgehog."

"Now what's a hedgehog exactly?" Ira was eyeing her full glass and his own empty one. "I get them mixed up with groundhogs and gophers."

"They're— Well, what does it matter if they are all wearing little polka-dotted clothes, vests and hats and things," she said irritably.

"I suppose," he said, now a little frightened. What was wrong with her? He did not like stressful moments in restaurants. They caused his mind to wander strangely to random thoughts like *Why are these things called* napkins *rather than* lapkins? or *I'll bet God really loves butter.* He tried to focus on the visuals, what she was wearing, which was a silk, pumpkin-colored blouse he hesitated complimenting her on lest she think he was gay. Marilyn had once threatened to call off their wedding because he had strenuously complimented the fabric of her gown and then had shopped too long and discontentedly for his own tuxedo, failing to find just the right shade of "mourning dove," a color he had read of in a wedding magazine. "Are you homosexual?" she had asked. "You must tell me now. I won't make the same mistake my sister did."

Perhaps Zora's irritability was only creative frustration. Ira understood. Though his position was with the Historical Soci-

ety's Human Resources Office, he liked to help with the society's exhibitions, doing posters and dioramas and once even
making a puppet for a little show the society had put on about
the first governor. Thank God for meaningful work! He understood those small, diaphanous artistic ambitions that overtook
people and could look like nervous breakdowns.

"What happens in your hedgehog tale?" Ira asked, then
settled in to finish up his dinner, eggplant parmesan that he
wished now he hadn't ordered. He was coveting Zora's wodge
of steak. Perhaps he had an iron deficiency. Or perhaps it was
just a desire for the taste of metal and blood in his mouth.
Zora, he knew, was committed to meat. While everyone else's
cars were busy protesting the prospect of war or supporting the
summoned troops, Zora's Honda had a bumper sticker that
said, RED MEAT IS NOT BAD FOR YOU. FUZZY, GREENISH BLUE
MEAT IS BAD FOR YOU.

"The hedgehog tale? Well," Zora began. "The hedgehog
goes for a walk, because he is feeling sad—it's based on a story
I used to tell my son. The hedgehog goes for a walk and comes
upon this strange yellow house that has a sign on it that says,
WELCOME, HEDGEHOG: THIS COULD BE YOUR NEW HOME, and
because he's been feeling sad, the thought of a new home
appeals. So he goes in and inside is a family of alligators—
Well, I'll spare you the rest, but you can get the general flavor
of it from that."

"I don't know about that family of alligators."

She was quiet for a minute, chewing her beautiful ruby
steak. "Every family is a family of alligators," she said.

"Well—that's certainly one way of looking at it." Ira glanced
at his watch.

"Yeah. To get back to the book. It gives me an outlet. I mean, my job's not terrible. Some of the kids are cute. But some are impossible, of course, some are disturbed, some are just spoiled and ill-behaved. It's hard to know what to do. We're not allowed to hit them."

"You're 'not allowed to hit them'?" He could see she had now made some progress with her wine.

"I'm from Kentucky," she said.

"Ah." He drank from his water glass, stalling.

She chewed thoughtfully. Merlot was beginning to etch a ragged, scabby line in the dead skin of her bottom lip. "It's like Ireland but with more horses and guns."

"Not a lot of Jews down there." He had no idea why he said half the things he said. Perhaps this time it was because he had once been a community-based historian, digging in archives for the genealogies and iconographies of various ethnic groups, not realizing that other historians generally thought this a sentimental form of history, shedding light on nothing; and though shedding light on nothing seemed not a bad idea to him, when it became available, he had taken the human resources job.

"Not too many," she said. "I did know an Armenian family growing up. At least I *think* they were Armenian."

When the check came, she ignored it, as if it were some fly that had landed and would soon be taking off again. So much for feminism. Ira pulled out his state-workers credit card and the waitress came by and whisked it away. There were, he was once told, four seven-word sentences that generally signaled the end of a relationship. The first was "I think we should see other people." (Which always meant another seven-word sentence: "I am already sleeping with someone else.") The second seven-word sentence was, reputedly, "Maybe you could just leave the tip." The third was "How could you again forget your wallet?" And the fourth, the killer of all killers, was "Oh, look, I've forgotten my wallet, too!"

He did not imagine they would ever see each other again. But when he dropped her off at her house, walking her to her door, Zora suddenly grabbed his face with both hands, and her mouth became its own wet creature exploring his. She opened up his jacket, pushing her body inside it, against his, the pumpkin-colored silk of her blouse slid upon his shirt. Her lips came away in a slurp. "I'm going to call you," she said, smiling. Her eyes were wild, as if with gin, though she had only been drinking wine.

"OK," he mumbled, walking backward down her steps, in the dark, his car still running, its headlights bright along her street.

He was in her living room the following week. It was beige and white with cranberry accents. On the walls were black-framed photos of her son, Bruno, from all ages, including now. There were pictures of Bruno lying prone on the ground. There were pictures of Bruno and Zora together, he hidden in the folds of her skirt, and she hanging her then-long hair down into his face, covering him completely. There he was again, leaning in between her knees, naked as a cello. There were pictures of him in the bath, though in some he was clearly already at the start of puberty. In the corner stood perhaps a dozen wooden sculptures of naked boys she had carved herself. "One of my hobbies, which I was telling you about," she said. They were astounding little things. She had drilled holes in their penises with a brace and bit to allow for water in case she could someday sell them as garden fountains. "These are winged boys. The beautiful adolescent boy who flies away. It's from mythology. I forget what they're called. I just love their little rumps." He nodded, studying the tight, sculpted buttocks, the spouted, mushroomy phalluses, the long backs and limbs. So: this was the sort of woman he'd been missing out on not being single all these years. What had he been thinking of staying married for so long?

He sat down and asked for wine. "You know, I'm just a little gun-shy romantically," he said apologetically. "I don't have the confidence I used to. I don't think I can even take my clothes off in front of another person. Not even at the gym, frankly. I've been changing in the toilet stalls. After divorce and all."

"Oh, divorce will do that to you totally," she said reassuringly. She poured him some wine. "It's like a trick. It's like someone puts a rug over a trapdoor and says, 'Stand there.' And so you do. Then boom." She took out a hashish pipe, lit it, sucking, then gave it to him.

"I've never seen a pediatrician smoke hashish before."

"Really?" she said, with some difficulty, her breath still sucked in.

The nipples of her breasts were long, cylindrical, and stiff, so that her chest looked somewhat as if two small sink plungers had flown across the room and suctioned themselves there. His mouth opened hungrily to kiss them.

"Perhaps you would like to take off your shoes," she whispered.

"Oh, not really," he said.

There was sex where you were looked in the eye and beautiful things were said to you, and then there was what Ira used to think of as yoo-hoo sex: where the other person seemed spirited away, not quite there, their pleasure mysterious and crazy and only accidentally involving you. "Yoo-hoo?" was what his grandmother always called before entering a house where she knew someone but not well enough to know whether they were actually home.

"Where *are* you?" Ira said in the dark. He decided in a case such as this he could feel a chaste and sanctifying distance. It wasn't he who was having sex. The condom was having sex and he was just trying to stop it. Zora's candles on the nightstand were heated to clear pools in their tins. They flickered smokily. He would try not to think about how before she had even lit them and pulled back the bedcovers he had noticed the candles were already melted down to the size of buttons, their wicks blackened to a crisp. It was not good to think about the previous burning of the bedroom candles of a woman who had just unzipped your pants. Besides, he was too grateful for the fact of those candles—especially with all those little wonder boys in the living room. Perhaps his whitening chest hair would not look so white. This was what candles were made for: the sad, sexually shy, out-of-shape, middle-aged him. How had he not understood this in marriage? Zora herself looked ageless, like a nymph with her short hair, although once she got Ira's glasses off, she became a blur of dim and shifting shapes and might as well have been Dick Cheney or Lon Chaney or Lee Marvin or the Blob, except that she smelled good and but for the occasional rough patch had the satiny skin of a girl.

She let out a long, spent sigh.

"Where did you go?" he asked again anxiously.

"I've been right here, silly," she said and pinched his hip. She lifted one of her long legs up and down outside the covers. "Did you get off?"

"I beg your pardon?"

"Did you get off?"

"'Get off'?" Someone else had once asked him the same question, when he'd stopped in the jetway to tie his shoe after debarking from a plane.

"Have an orgasm? With some men it's not always clear."

"Yes, thank you, I mean, it was—to me—very clear."

"You're still wearing your wedding ring," she said.

"It's stuck, I don't know why—"

"Let me get at that thing," she said and pulled hard on his finger, but the loose skin around his knuckle bunched up and blocked it.

"Ow," he finally said. His skin was abraded.

"Perhaps later with soap," she said. She lay back and swung her legs up in the air again.

"Do you like to dance?" he asked.

"Sometimes," she said.

"I'll bet you're a wonderful dancer," said Ira.

"Not really," she said. "But I can always think of things to do."

"That's a nice trait."

"You think so?" she asked, and she leaned in and began tickling him.

"I don't think I'm that ticklish," he said.

"Oh." She stopped.

"I mean, I'm probably a *little*," he added, "just not a lot."

"I would like you to meet my son," she said.

"Is he here?"

"He's under the bed. Bruny?" Oh, these funny ones were funny.

"What is his name?"

"Bruno. I call him Bruny. He's with his dad this week."

The extended families of divorce. Ira tried not to feel jealous. It was quite possible he was not mature enough to date a divorced woman. "Tell me about his dad."

"His dad? His dad is another pediatrician, but he was really into English country dancing. Where eventually he met a lass. Alas."

Ira would write that down in his book. *Alas, a lass.* "I don't think anyone should dance in a way that's not just regular dancing," said Ira. "It's not normal. That's just my opinion."

"Well, he left a long time ago. He said he'd made a terrible mistake getting married. He said that he just wasn't capable of intimacy. I know that's true for some people, but I had never actually heard anyone say that out loud about themselves."

"I know!" said Ira. "Even Hitler never said that! I mean, I don't mean to compare your ex to Hitler *as a leader.* Only as a man."

Zora stroked his arm. "Do you feel ready to meet Bruno? I mean, he didn't care for my last boyfriend at all. That's why we broke up."

"Really?" This silenced Ira for a moment. "If I left those matters to my daughter, I'd be dating a beagle."

"I believe children come first." Her voice now had a steely edge.

"Oh, yes, yes, so do I," he said quickly. He felt suddenly paralyzed and cold.

She reached into the nightstand drawer, took out a vial, and bit into a pill. "Here, take half," she said. "Otherwise we won't get any sleep at all. Sometimes I snore. Probably you do, too."

"This is so cute," Ira said warmly. "Our taking these pills together."

He staggered through his days, tired and unsure. At the office he misplaced files. Sometimes he knocked things over by accident—a glass of water or the benefits manual. News of the coming war, too, was taking its toll. He lay in bed at night, the moments before sleep a kind of stark acquaintance with death. What had happened to the world? March still did not look completely like spring, especially with the plastic sheeting duct-taped to his windows. When he tried to look out, the trees seemed to be pasted onto the waxy dinge of a wintry-looking sky. He wished this month had a less military verb for a name. Why March? How about a month named Skip? That could work.

He got two cats from the pound so that Bekka could have some live pet action at his house, too. He and Bekka went to the store and stocked up on litter and cat food.

"Provisions!" exclaimed Ira.

"In case the war comes here, we can eat the cat food," suggested Bekka.

"Cat food, heck. We can eat the cats," said Ira.

"That's disgusting, Dad."

Ira shrugged.

"You see, that's one of the things Mom didn't like about you!" she added.

"Really? She said that?"

"Sort of."

"Mom likes me. She's just very busy."

"Whatever."

He got back to the cats. "What should we name them?" One should always name food.

"I don't know." Bekka studied the cats.

Ira hated the precious literary names people gave pets—characters from opera and Proust. When he'd first met Marilyn, she had a cat named Portia, but Ira had insisted on calling it Fang.

"I think we should name them Snowball and Snowflake," said Bekka, looking glassy-eyed at the two golden tabbies.

"They don't look like a snowball or a snowflake," said Ira, trying not to let his disappointment show. Sometimes Bekka seemed completely banal to him. She had spells of inexplicable and vapid conventionality. He had always wanted to name a cat Bowser. "How about Bowser?" In the pound someone with name tag duty had named them "Jake" and "Fake Jake," but the quotation marks around their names seemed an invitation to change them.

"Fireball and Fireflake," Bekka tried again.

Ira looked at her, he hoped, beseechingly and persuasively. "*Really?* Fireball and Fireflake don't really sound like cats that would belong to you."

Bekka's face clenched tearily. "You don't know me! I live with you only part-time! The other part of the time I live with Mom, and she doesn't know me either! The only person who knows me is me!"

"OK, OK," said Ira. The cats were eyeing him warily. In

time of war never argue with a fireball or a fireflake. Never argue with the food. "Fireball and Fireflake." What were those? Two lonely middle-aged people on a date.

"Why don't you come to dinner?" Zora phoned one afternoon. "I'm making spring spaghetti, Bruny's favorite, and you can come over and meet him. Unless you have Bekka tonight."

"No, I don't," Ira said mournfully. "What is spring spaghetti?"

"Oh, it's the same as regular spaghetti, you just serve it kind of lukewarm. Room temperature. With a little fresh basil."

"What should I bring?"

"Oh, perhaps you could just bring a small appetizer and some dessert," she said. "And maybe a salad, some bread if you're close to a bakery, and a bottle of wine. Also an extra chair, if you have one. We'll need an extra chair."

"OK," he said.

He was a litttle loaded down at the door. She stepped outside, he thought to help him, but she simply put her arms around him and kissed him. "I have to kiss you now here outdoors. Bruny doesn't like to see that sort of thing." She kissed Ira in a sweet, rubbery way on the mouth. Then she stepped back in, smiling, holding the door open for him. Oh, the beautiful smiles of the insane. Soon, he was sure, there would be a study that showed that the mentally ill were actually more attractive than other people. Dating proved it! The aluminum foil over his salad was sliding off and the brownies he had made for dessert were still warm and underneath the salad bowl were probably heating and wilting the lettuce. He attempted a familiar and proprietary stride through her living room, though he felt neither, then dumped everything on her kitchen table.

"Oh, thank you," she said and placed her hand on the small of his back. He was deeply attracted to her. There was nothing he could do about that.

"It smells good," he said. "You smell good." Some mix of garlic and citrus and baby powder overlaid with nutmeg. Her hand wandered down and stroked his behind. "I've got to run out to the car and get the appetizer and the chair," he said and made a quick dash. When he came back in, handed her the appetizer—a dish of herbed olives (he knew nothing about food; someone at work had told him you could never go wrong with herbed olives: "Spell it out—h-e-r b-e-d. Get it?")—and then set the chair up at Zora's little dining table for two (he'd never seen one not set up for at least four), Zora looked brightly at him and whispered, "Are you ready to meet Bruny?"

Ready. He did not know precisely what she meant by that. It seemed she had reversed everything, that she should be asking Bruno, or Bruny, or Brune, if he was ready to meet *him*. "Ready," he said.

There was wavery flute music from behind a closed door down the hallway. "Bruny?" Zora called. The music stopped. Suddenly a barking, howling voice called *"What?"*

"Come out and meet Ira, please."

There was silence. There was nothing. Nobody moved at all for a very long time. Ira smiled politely. "Oh, let him play," he said.

"I'll be right back," said Zora, and she headed down the hall to Bruno's room, knocked on the door, then went in, closing it behind her. Ira stood there for a while, then he picked up the Screwpull, opened the bottle of wine, and began to drink. After several minutes Zora returned to the kitchen, sighing. "Bruny's in a bit of a mood." Suddenly a door slammed and loud, trudging footsteps brought Bruno, the boy himself, into the kitchen. He was barefoot and in a T-shirt and gym shorts, his legs already darkening with hair. His eyebrows sprouted in a manly black V over the bridge of his nose. He was not tall, but he was muscular already, broad-shouldered and thick-limbed, and he folded his arms across his chest and leaned against the wall in weary belligerence.

"Bruny, this is Ira," said Zora. Ira put his wineglass down and thrust out his hand to introduce himself. Bruno unfolded his arms but did not shake hands. Instead, he thrust out his chin and scowled. Ira picked up his wineglass again.

"So, good to meet you. Your mother has said a lot of wonderful things about you." He tried to remember one.

Bruno looked at the appetizer bowl. "What's this grassy gunk all over the olives." It was not really a question, so no one answered it. Bruno turned back to his mother. "May I go back to my room now?"

"Yes, dear," said Zora. She looked at Ira. "He's practicing for the woodwind competition next Saturday. He's very serious."

When Bruno had tramped back down to his room, Ira leaned in to kiss Zora, but she pulled away. "Bruny might hear us," she whispered.

"Let's go to a restaurant. Just you and me. My salad's no good."

"Oh, we couldn't leave Bruno here alone. He's only sixteen."

"I was working in a steel factory when I was sixteen!" Ira decided not to say. Instead he said, "Doesn't he have friends?"

"He's between social groups right now," Zora said defensively. "It's difficult for him to find other kids who are as intellectually serious as he is."

"We'll rent him a movie," said Ira. "Excuse me, a *film*. A foreign film, since he's serious. A documentary. We'll rent him a foreign documentary!"

"We don't have a VCR."

"You don't have a VCR?" At this point Ira found the silverware and helped set the table. When they sat down to eat and poured more wine in their glasses, Bruno suddenly came out and joined them, with no beckoning. The spring spaghetti was tossed in a large glass bowl with grated cheese. "Just how you like it, Brune," said Zora.

"So, Bruno. What grade are you in?"

Bruno rolled his eyes. "Tenth," he said.

"So college is a ways off, " said Ira, accidentally thinking out loud.

"I guess," said Bruno, who then tucked into the spring spaghetti.

"So—what classes are you taking in school, besides music?" asked Ira, after a long awkward spell.

"I don't take music," he said with his mouth full. "I'm in All-State Woodwinds."

"All-State Woodwinds! Interesting! Do you take any courses in like, say, American history?"

"They're studying the Amazon rain forest yet again," said Zora. "They've been studying it since preschool."

Ira slurped with morose heartiness at his wine—he had spent too much of his life wandering about in the desert of his own drool, oh, the mealtime assaults he had made on his own fragile consciousness—and some dribbled on his shirt. "For Pete's sake, look at this." He dabbed at the wine spot with his napkin and looked up at Bruno, with an ingratiating grin. "Someday this could happen to you," Ira said, twinkling in Bruno's direction.

"That would never happen to me," muttered Bruno.

Ira continued dabbing at his shirt. He began thinking of his book. *Though I be your mother's beau, no rival I, no foe, faux foe.* He loved rhymes. *Fum! Thumb! Dumb!* They were harmonious and joyous in the face of total crap.

Bruno began gently kicking his mother under the table. Zora began playfully to nudge him back, and soon they were both kicking away, their energetic footsie causing them to slip in their chairs a little, while Ira pretended not to notice, cutting his salad with the edge of his fork, too frightened to look up very much. After a few minutes—when the footsie had stopped and Ira had exclaimed, "Great dinner, Zora!"—they all stood and cleared their places, taking the dishes into the kitchen, putting them in a messy pile in the sink. Ira started halfheartedly to run warm water over them, and Zora and Bruno, some distance behind him, began to jostle up against each other, ramming lightly into each other's sides. Ira glanced over his shoulder and saw Zora now step back and assume a wrestler's starting stance, as Bruno leaped toward her, heaving her over his shoulder, then running her into the living room, where, Ira could see, Bruno dumped her, laughing, on the couch.

Should Ira join in? Should he leave?

"I can still pin you, Brune, when we're on the bed," Zora said.

"Yeah, right," said Bruno.

Perhaps it was time to go. Next time Ira would bring over a VCR for Bruno and just take Zora out to eat. "Well, look at the time! Good to meet you, Bruno," he said, shaking the kid's large, limp hand. Zora stood breathlessly. She walked Ira out to his car, helping to carry his chair and salad bowl. "It was a lovely dinner," said Ira. "And you are a lovely woman. And your son seems so bright and the two of you are adorable together."

Zora beamed, seemingly mute with happiness. If only Ira had known how to speak such fanciful baubles during his marriage, surely Marilyn would never have left him.

He gave Zora a quick kiss on the cheek—the heat of her wrestling had heightened her beautiful nutmeg smell—then kissed her again on the neck, near her ear. Alone in the car on the way home he thought of all the deeply wrong erotic attachments made in wartime, all the crazy romances cooked up quickly by the species to offset death. He turned the radio on: the news of the Mideast was so surreal and bleak that when he heard the tonnage of the bombs planned for Baghdad, he could feel his jaw fall slack in astonishment. He pulled the car over, turned on the interior light, and gazed in the rearview mirror just to see what his face looked like in this particular state. He had felt his face drop in this manner once before—when he got the divorce papers from Marilyn, now *there* was shock and awe for you; there was *decapitation*—but he had never actually seen what he looked like this way. So. Now he knew. Not good: stunned, pale, and not all that bright. It wasn't the same as self-knowledge, but life was long and not that edifying, and one sometimes had to make do with randomly seized tidbits.

He started up again, slowly; outside it had begun to rain, and at a brightly lit intersection of two gas stations, one QuikTrip,

and a KFC, half a dozen young people in hooded yellow slick-
ers were holding up signs that read HONK FOR PEACE. Ira fell
upon his horn, first bouncing his hand there, then just leaning
his whole arm into it. Other cars began to do the same, and
soon no one was going anywhere, a congregation of mourning
doves! but honking like geese in a wild chorus of futility, windshield wipers clearing their fan-shaped spaces on the drizzled
night glass. No car went anywhere for the change of two lights.
For all its stupidity and solipsism and scenic civic grief, it was
something like a gorgeous moment.

Despite her reading difficulties, despite the witless naming of
the cats, Ira knew Bekka was highly intelligent. He knew from
the time she spent lying around the house, bored and sighing,
saying, "Dad? When will childhood be over?" This was a sign
of genius! As were other things. Her complete imperviousness
to the adult male voice, for instance. Her scrutiny of all food.
With interest and hesitancy, she studied the antiwar lawn signs
that bestrewed the neighborhood. WAR IS NOT THE PATH TO
PEACE, she read slowly aloud. Then added, "Well duh."
    WAR IS NOT THE ANSWER, she read on another. "Well that
doesn't make sense," she said to Ira. "War *is* the answer," she
said. "It's the answer to the question What's George Bush going
to do real soon?"
    The times Bekka stayed at Ira's house, she woke up in the
morning and told him her dreams. "I had a dream last night
that I was walking with two of my friends and we met a wolf.
But I made a deal with the wolf. I said, 'Don't eat me. These
other two have more meat on them.' And the wolf said, 'OK,'
and we shook on it and I got away."

Or "I had a strange dream last night that I was a bad little fairy."

She was in contact with her turmoil and with her ability to survive. How could that be anything less than emotional brilliance?

One morning she said, "I had a really scary dream. There was this tornado with a face inside? And I married it." Ira smiled. "It may sound funny to you, Dad, but it was really scary."

He stole a look at her school writing journal once and found this poem:

Time moving.
Time standing still.
What is the difference?
Time standing still is the difference.

He had no idea what it meant, but he knew it was awesome. He had given her the middle name Clio, after the muse of History, so of course she would know very well that time standing still *was* the difference—whatever that meant. He himself felt he was watching history from the dimmest of backwaters, a land of beer and golf, the horizon peacefully fish-gray, the sky a suicide silver, the windows duct-taped with plastic sheeting so that he felt he was observing life from a plastic container, like a leftover, peering into the tallow fog of the world. *Time moving. Time standing still.*

The major bombing started on the first day of spring. "It's happening," Ira said into Mike's answering machine. "The whole thing is starting now."

Zora called and asked him to the movies. "Sure," Ira said. "I'd love to."

"Well, we were thinking of this Arnold Schwarzenegger movie, but Bruno would also be willing to see the Mel Gibson one." *We.* He was dating a tenth grader now. Even in tenth grade he'd never done that. Well, now he'd see what he'd been missing.

They picked him up at six-forty, and, as Bruno made no move to cede the front seat, Ira sat in the back of Zora's Honda, his long legs wedged together at a diagonal like a lady riding sidesaddle. Zora drove carefully, not like a mad hellcat at all, which for some reason he'd thought she would. As a result they were late for the Mel Gibson movie and had to make do with the Arnold Schwarzenegger one. Ira thrust money at the ticket taker saying, "Three please," and they all wordlessly went in, their computerized stubs in hand. "So you like Arnold Schwarze-negger?" Ira said to Bruno as they headed down one of the red-carpeted corridors.

"Not really," muttered Bruno. Bruno sat between Zora and Ira, and together they all passed a small container of popcorn back and forth. Ira jumped up twice to refill it back out in the lobby, a kind of relief for him from Arnold, whose line read-ings were less brutish than they used to be, but not less brutish enough. Afterward, heading out into the parking lot, Bruno and Zora reenacted body-bouncing scenes from the film, throwing themselves against each other's backs and shoulders with great, giggling force. When they reached the car, Ira was again relegated to the backseat.

"Shall we go to dinner?" he called up to the front.

Both Zora and Bruno were silent.

"Shall we?" he tried again cheerfully.

"Would you like to, Bruno?" asked Zora. "Are you hungry?"

"I don't know," Bruno said, peering gloomily out the window.

"Did you like the movie?" asked Ira.

Bruno shrugged. "I dunno."

They went to a barbecue place and got ribs and chicken. "Let me pay for this," said Ira, though Zora had never offered. He would spare them the awkwardness.

"Oh, OK," she said.

Afterward, Zora dropped Ira at the curb, where Ira stood for a minute, waving, in front of his house. Bruno flung the back of his hand toward him, not actually looking. Zora waved vigorously through the open window over the top of the car. He watched them roll down the end of the block and disappear around the corner. He went inside and made himself a drink with cranberry juice and rum. He turned on the TV news and watched the bombing. Night bombing, so you could not really see.

A few mornings later was the first of a new month, his birthday month. The illusion of time flying, he knew, was to make people think life could have more in it than it actually could. Actually, time flying could make human lives seem victorious over time itself. Time flew so fast that in ways it failed to make an impact. People's lives fell between its stabbing powers like insects between raindrops. "We cheat the power of time with our very brevity!" he said aloud to Bekka, feeling confident she would understand, but she only just kept petting the cats. The

house had already begun to fill with the acrid-honey smell of
cat pee, though neither he nor Bekka seemed to mind. Spring!
One more month and it would be May, his least favorite. Why
not a month named Can? Or Must! Well, maybe not Must.
Zora phoned him early, with a dour tone. "I don't know. I
think we should break up," she said.

"You do?"

"Yes, I don't see that this is going anywhere. Things aren't
really moving forward in any way I can understand. And I
don't think we should waste each other's time."

"Really?" Desperation washed through him.

"It may be fine for some, but dinner, movie, then sex is not
my idea of a relationship."

"Maybe we could eliminate the movie?"

"We're adults—"

"True. I mean, we are?"

"—and what is the point, if there are clear obstacles or any
unclear idea of where this is headed, of continuing? It becomes
difficult to maintain faith. We've hardly begun seeing each
other, I realize, but already I just don't envision us as a couple."

"I'm sorry to hear you say that." He was now sitting down in
his kitchen. He could feel himself trying not to cry.

"Let's just move on," she said with gentle firmness.

"Really? Is that honestly what you think? I feel terrible."

"April Fools'!" she cried out into the phone.

His heart rose to his throat, then sank to his colon, then
bobbed back up close to the surface of his rib cage, where his
right hand was clutching at it. Were there paddles somewhere
close by that could be applied to his chest?

"I beg your pardon?" he asked faintly.

"April Fools'," she said again, laughing. "It's April Fools' Day."

"I guess," he said, gasping a little, "I guess that's the kind of joke that gets better the longer you think about it."

He had never been involved with the mentally ill before, but he now felt more than ever that there should be strong international laws against them being too good-looking.

"How are you liking Zora?" asked Mike over a beer, after work, after they'd mulled over the war and Dick Cheney's tax return, which had just been reprinted in the paper. Why wasn't there a revolution? Was everyone too distracted with tennis and sex and iris bulbs? Marxism in the spring lacked oomph. Ira had just hired someone to paint his house, so that now in his front lawn he had two signs: WAR IS NOT THE ANSWER in blue and on the other side, in black and yellow, JENKINS PAINTING IS THE ANSWER.

"Oh, Zora's great." Ira paused. "Great. Just great. In fact, do you perhaps know any other single women?"

"Really?"

"Well, it's just that she might not be all that mentally *well*." Ira thought about the moment, just last night, at dinner, when she'd said, "I love your mouth most when it does that odd grimace in the middle of sex," and then she contorted her face so hideously, Ira felt he had been struck. Later in the evening she had said, "Watch this," and she took her collapsible umbrella, placed its handle on the crotch of her trousers, then pressed the button that sent it rocketing out, unfurled, like a cartoon erection. Ira did not know who or what she was, though he wanted to cut her slack, give her a break, bestow upon her the benefit of the doubt—all those paradoxical clichés of supposed generosity, most of which he had denied his wife. He tried not to think that the only happiness he might have been fated for had already occurred, had been with Bekka and Marilyn, when the three of them were together. A hike, a bike ride—he tried not to think that his crazy dream of family had shown its sweet face only long enough to torment him for the rest of his life though scarcely long enough to sustain him through a meal. To torture oneself with this idea of family happiness while not actually having a family, he decided, might be a fairly new circumstance in social history. People were probably not like this a hundred years ago. He imagined an exhibit at the society. He imagined the puppets.

"Sanity's conjectural," said Mike. His brow furrowed thoughtfully. "Zora's very attractive, don't you think?"

Ira thought of her beautiful, slippery skin, the dark, sweet hair, the lithe sylph's body, the mad, hysterical laugh. She had once, though only briefly, insisted that Man Ray and Ray Charles were brothers. "She is attractive," Ira said. "But you say that like it's a good thing."

"Right now," said Mike, "I feel like anything that isn't about killing people is a good thing."

"This may be about that," said Ira.

"Oh, I see. Now we're entering the callow, glib part of spring."

"She's wack, as the kids say."

Mike looked confused. "Is that like wacko?"

"It's like wacko, but not like *Waco*—at least I don't think so. At least not yet. I would stop seeing her, but I don't seem to be able to. Especially now with all that's happening in the world,

I can't live without some intimacy, companionship, whatever you want to call it, to face down this global craziness."

"You shouldn't use people as human shields." Mike paused. "Or—I don't know—maybe you should."

"I can't let go of hope, of the illusion of something coming out of this romance, I'm sorry. Divorce is a trauma, believe me, I know. Its pain is a national secret! But that's not it. I can't let go of love. I can't live without love in my life. Hold my hand," said Ira. His eyes were starting to water. Once when he was a small child he had gotten lost, and when his mother had finally found him, four blocks from home, she had asked him if he had been scared. "Not really," he had said, sniffling pridefully. "But then my eyes just suddenly started to water."

"I beg your pardon?" asked Mike.

"I can't believe I just asked you to hold my hand," said Ira, but Mike had already taken it.

The hashish was good. The sleeping pills were good. He was walking slowly around the halls at work in what was a combination of serene energy and a nap. With his birthday coming up, he went to the doctor for his triennial annual physical and, mentioning a short list of nebulous symptoms, he was given dismissive diagnoses of "benign vertigo," "pseudo gout," and perhaps "migraine aura," the names, no doubt, of rock bands. "You've got the pulse of a boy, and the mind of a boy, too," said his doctor, an old golfing friend.

Health, Ira decided, was notional. Palm Sunday—all these *goyim* festivals were preprinted on his calendar—was his birthday, and when Zora called he blurted out that information.

"It is?" she said. "You old man! Are you feeling undernookied? I'll come over Sunday and read your palm. If you know what I mean." Wasn't she cute? Dammit, she was cute. She arrived with Bruno and a chocolate cake in tow. "Happy birthday," she said. "Bruno helped me make the frosting."

"Did you now," Ira said to Bruno, patting him on the back in a brotherly embrace that the boy attempted to duck and slide out from under.

They ordered Chinese food and talked about high school, Advanced Placement courses, homeroom teachers, and James Galway (soulful mick or soulless dork, who could decide?). Zora brought out the cake. There were no candles so Ira lit a match, stuck it upright in the frosting, and blew it out. His wish had been a vague and general one of good health for Bekka. No one but her. He had put nobody else in his damn wish. Not the Iraqi people; not the GIs; not Mike, who had held his hand; not Zora. This kind of focused intensity was bad for the planet.

"Shall we sit on Bruno?" Zora was laughing and backing her sweet tush into Bruno, who was now sprawled out on Ira's sofa, resting. "Come on!" she called to Ira. "Let's sit on Bruno." She was now sitting on the boy's hip while Bruno protested in a laughing, grunting manner.

At this point Ira was making his way toward the liquor cabinet. He believed there was some bourbon there. He would not need ice. "Would you care for some bourbon?" he called over to Zora, who was now wrestling with Bruno and looked up at Ira and said nothing. Bruno, too, looked at him and said nothing.

Ira continued to pour. Zora straightened up and walked over to him. He was both drinking bourbon and eating cake. He had a pancreas like a rock. "We should probably go," said Zora. "It's a school night."

"Oh, OK," said Ira, swallowing. "I mean, I wish you didn't have to."

"School. What can you do? I'm going to take the rest of the cake home for Bruny's lunch tomorrow. It's his favorite."

Heat and sorrow filled Ira. The cake had been her only present to him. He closed his eyes and nuzzled his face into hers. "Not now," she whispered. "He gets upset."

"Oh," Ira said. "Well, then I'll walk you out to the car." And there he gave her a quick hug. She walked around the car and got in on the driver's side. He stepped back up on the curb and knocked on the window of the passenger's side to say good-bye to Bruno. But the boy would not turn. He flipped his hand up, showing Ira the back of it.

"Bye! Thank you for sharing my birthday with me!" Ira called out. Where affection fell on its ass, politeness could step up. But then there was the heat and sorrow again just filling his face. Zora's Honda lights went on, then the engine, then the whole vehicle flew down the street.

At Bekka's coo-coo private school, to which Marilyn had years ago insisted on sending her, the students and teachers were assiduously avoiding talk of the war. In Bekka's class they were doing finger-knitting while simultaneously discussing their hypothetical stock market investments. The class was doing best with preferred stock in Kraft, GE, and GM; watching their investments move slightly every morning on the Dow Jones was also helping their little knitted scarves. It was a

right-brain, left-brain thing. For this, Ira forked over nine thousand dollars a year. Not that he really cared. As long as she was
in a place safe from war—the alerts were moving from orange
to red to orange; no information, just duct tape and bright,
mind-wrecking colors—turning Bekka into a knitting stock-
broker was OK with him. *Exploit the system, man!* he himself
used to say, in college. He could, however, no longer watch TV.
He packed it up, along with the VCR, and brought the whole
thing over to Zora's. "Here," he said. "This is for Bruno."

"You are so nice," she said, and kissed him near his ear and
then on his ear. Possibly he was madly in love with her.

"The TV's broken," said Ira, when Bekka came that weekend and asked about it. "It's in the shop."

"Whatever," Bekka said, pulling her scarf yarn along the
floor so the cats could play.

When next he picked Zora up to go out, she said, "Come on
in. Bruno's watching a movie on your VCR."

"Does he like it? Should I say hello to him?"

Zora shrugged. "If you want."

He stepped into the house, but the TV was not in the living
room. It was in Zora's bedroom, where, spread out half-naked
on Zora's bedspread, as he himself had been just a few evenings
before, lay Bruno. He was watching Bergman's *The Magic Flute*.

"Hi, Brune," he said. The boy said nothing, transfixed, perhaps not hearing him. Zora came in and pressed a cold glass of
water against the back of Bruno's thigh.

"Yow!" cried Bruno.

"Here's your water," said Zora, walking her fingers up one
of his legs.

Bruno took the glass and placed it on the floor. The singing on the same television screen that had so recently brought Ira the fiery bombing of Baghdad seemed athletic and absurd, perhaps a kind of joke. But Bruno remained riveted. "Well, enjoy the show," said Ira, who didn't really expect to be thanked for the TV, though now actually knowing he wouldn't be made him feel a little crestfallen.

On the way back out Ira again noticed the sculptures in the corner of the living room. Zora had added two new ones. They were more abstract, made entirely out of old recorders and other woodwinds, but were recognizably boys, priapic with piccolos. "A flute would have been too big," explained Zora, shortly after Ira had said, "So . . . you've been doing some new work!"

At the restaurant the sound system was playing Nancy Wilson singing "For All We Know." The walls, like love, were *trompe l'oeil*—walls painted as viewful windows, though only a fool wouldn't know they were walls. The menu, like love, was full of delicate, gruesome things—cheeks, tongues, thymus glands. The candle, like love, flickered—in the brass tops of the sugar bowl and salt and pepper shakers. He tried to capture Zora's gaze, which seemed to be darting around the room. "It's so nice to be here with you," he said. She turned and fixed him with a smile, repaired him with it. She was a gentle, lovely woman. Something in him kept coming stubbornly back to that. Here they were two lonely adults in a crazy world lucky to have found each other even if it was just for the time being. But now tears were drizzling down her face. Her mouth, collecting them in its corners, was retreating into a pinch.

"Oh, no, what's the matter?" He reached for her hand, but she pulled it away to hide her eyes behind it.

"I just miss Bruny," she said.

He could feel his heart go cold, despite himself. Oh, well. Tomorrow was Easter. All would rise from the dead.

"Don't you think he's fine?"

"It's just—I don't know. It's probably just me coming off my antidepressants."

"You've been on antidepressants?" he asked sympathetically.

"Yes, I was."

"You were on them when I first met you?" Maybe he had wandered into a whole *Flowers for Algernon* thing.

"Yes, indeed. I went on them two years ago, after my so-called 'nervous breakdown.'" And here she put two fingers in the air, to do quotation marks, but all of her fingers inadvertently sprang up and her hands clawed the air.

He didn't know what he should say. "Would you like me to take you home?"

"No, no, no. Oh, maybe you should. I'm sorry. It's just I feel I have so little time with him now. He's growing up so fast. I just wish I could go back in time." She blew her nose.

"I know what you mean."

"You know, once I was listening to some friends talk about traveling in the Pacific. They left Australia early one morning and arrived in California the evening of the day before. And I thought, I'd like to do that—keep crossing the international date line and get all the way back to when Bruno was a little boy again."

"Yeah," said Ira. "I'd like to get back to that moment where I signed my divorce agreement. I have a few changes I'd like to make."

"You'd have to bring a pen," she said strangely.

He studied her, to memorize her face. "I would never time-travel without a pen," he said.

She paused. "You look worried," she said. "You shouldn't do that with your forehead. It makes you look old." Then she began to sob.

He found her coat and took her home and walked her to the door. Above the house the hammered nickel of the moon gave off its murky shine. "It's a hard time in the world right now," Ira said. "It's hard on everybody. Go in and make yourself a good stiff drink. People don't drink the way they used to. That's what started this whole Iraq thing to begin with: it's a war of teetotalers. People have got to get off their wagons and their high horses and—" He kissed her forehead. "I'll call you tomorrow," he said, though he wouldn't. She squeezed his arm and said, "Sleep well." As he backed out of her driveway, he could see through her front bedroom window, where the TV was firing its colorful fire and Bruno was laid out in a shirtless stupor. Ira could see Zora come in, sit down, cuddle close to Bruno, put her arm around him, and rest her head on his shoulder.

Ira brusquely swung the car away, down the street. Was this *his* problem? Was he too old-fashioned? He had always thought he was a modern man. He knew, for instance, how to stop and ask for directions! And he did it a lot! Of course, afterward, he would sometimes stare at the guy and say, "Who the hell told you that bullshit?"

He had his limitations.

He had not gone to a single seder this week, for which he was glad. It seemed a bad time to attend a ceremony that gave thanks in any way for the slaughter of Middle Eastern boys. He had done that last year. He headed instead to the nearest bar, a dank, noisy dive called Sparky's, where he used to go just after Marilyn left him. When he was married he never drank, but after he was divorced, he used to come in even in the mornings for beer, toast, and fried side meat. All his tin-penny miseries and chickenshit joys would lead him once again to Sparky's. Those half-dozen times he had run into Marilyn at a store—this small town!—he had felt like a dog seeing its owner. Here was the person he knew best in life, squeezing an avocado and acting like she didn't see him. *Oh, here I am, oh, here I am!* But in Sparky's, he knew, he was safe from such unexpected encounters, and after any such unexpected encounters he had often come here. He could sit alone and moan to Sparky. Some people consulted Marcus Aurelius for philosophy about the pain of existence. Ira consulted Sparky. Sparky himself didn't actually have that much to say about the pain of existence. He mostly leaned across the bar, drying a smudgy glass with a dingy towel, and said, "Choose life!" then guffawed.

"Bourbon straight up," said Ira, picking the bar stool closest to the TV so that war news would be hardest to watch from there. Or so he hoped. He let the sharp, buttery elixir of the bourbon warm his mouth, then swallowed its neat, sweet heat. He did this over and over, ordering drink after drink, until he was lit to the gills. At which point he looked up and saw there were other people gathered at the bar, each alone on a chrome-and-vinyl stool, doing the same. "Happy Easter," Ira said to them, lifting his glass with his left hand, the one with the wedding ring still jammed on. "The dead shall rise! The dead are risen! The damages will be mitigated! The Messiah is back among us squeezing the flesh—that nap went by quickly, eh? May all the dead arise! No one has really been killed at all—OK, God looked away for a second to watch some *I Love Lucy* reruns, but he is back now. Nothing has been lost. All is restored. He watching over Israel, slumbers not nor sleeps!"

"Somebody slap that guy," said the man in the blue shirt at the end.

THE JUNIPER TREE

The night Robin Ross was dying in the hospital, I was waiting for a man to come pick me up—a man she had once dated, months before I began dating him—and he was late and I was wondering whether his going to see her with me was even wise. Perhaps I should go alone. Her colleague ZJ had called that morning and said, "Things are bad. When she leaves the hospital, she's not going home."

"I'll go see her tonight," I said. I felt I was a person of my word, and by saying something I would make it so. It was less like integrity perhaps and more like magic.

"That's a good idea," ZJ said. He was chairman of the theater department and had taken charge, like a husband, since Robin had asked him to; his tearfulness about her fate had already diminished. In the eighties he had lost a boyfriend to AIDS, and now all the legal and medical decision-making these last few months, he said, seemed numbingly familiar.

But then I found myself waiting, and soon it was seven-thirty and then eight and I imagined Robin was tired and sleeping in her metal hospital bed and would have more energy in the morning. When the man I was waiting for came, I said, "You know? It's so late. Maybe I should visit Robin in the morning when she'll have more energy and be more awake. The tumor presses on the skull, poor girl, and makes her groggy."

"Whatever you think is best," said the man. When I told him

what ZJ had said, that when Robin left the hospital, she wasn't
going home, the man looked puzzled. "Where is she going to
go?" He hadn't dated Robin very long, only a few weeks, and
had never really understood her. "Her garage was a pigsty," he
had once said. "I couldn't believe all the crap that was in it!"
And I had nodded agreeably, feeling I had won him; my own
garage wasn't that great, but whatever. I had triumphed over
others by dint of some unknowable charm. Now I was coming
to realize that a lot of people baffled this guy, and that I would
be next to become incomprehensible and unattractive. That
was how dating among straight middle-aged women seemed to
go in this college town: one available man every year or so just
made the rounds of us all. "I can share. I'm good at sharing,"
Robin used to say, laughing.

"Well I'm not," I said. "I'm not good at it in the least."

"It's late," I said again to the man, and I made two gin rickeys and lit candles.

Every woman I knew here drank—daily. In rejecting the
lives of our mothers, we found ourselves looking for stray volts
of mother love in the very places they could never be found:
gin, men, the college, our own mothers, and one another. I was
the only one of my friends—all of us academic transplants, all
soldiers of art stationed on a far-off base (or, so we imagined
it)—who hadn't had something terrible happen to her yet.

The next morning I dressed in cheery colors. Orange and
gold. There was nothing useful to bring Robin, but I made a
bouquet of cut mums nonetheless and stuck them in a plastic
cup with some wet paper towels holding them in. I was headed
toward the front door when the phone rang. It was ZJ. "I'm
leaving now to see Robin," I said.

"Don't bother."

"Oh, no," I said. My vision left me for a second.

"She died late last night. About two in the morning."

I sank down into a chair and my plastic cup of mums fell, breaking two stems. "Oh, my God," I said.

"I know," he said.

"I was going to go see her last night, but it got late and I thought it would be better to go this morning when she was more rested." I tried not to wail.

"Don't worry about it," he said.

"I feel terrible," I cried, as if this were what mattered.

"She was not doing well. It's a blessing." From diagnosis to decline had been precipitous, I knew. She was teaching, then suddenly the new chemo was not going well and she was lying outside of the emergency room, on the concrete, afraid to lie down inside because of other people's germs. Then she was placed in the actual hospital, which was full of other people's germs. She'd been there almost a week and I hadn't gotten in to see her.

"It's all so unbelievable."

"I know."

"How are *you*?" I asked.

"I can't even go there," he said.

"Please phone me if there's something I can do," I said emptily. "Let me know when the service will be."

"Sure," he said.

I went upstairs and with all my cheery clothes on got back into bed. It still smelled a little of the man. I pulled the sheet over my head and lay there, every muscle of my body strung taut. I could not move.

But I must have fallen asleep, and for some time, because when I heard the doorbell downstairs and pulled the sheet off my face, it was already dark, though the sun set these days at four, so it was hard ever to know by just looking out the windows what time it might possibly be. I flicked on the lights as I went—bedroom, hall, stairs—making my way down toward the ringing bell. I turned on the porch light and opened the door.

There stood Isabel and Pat. "We've got the gin, we've got the rickey mix," they said, holding up bags. "Come on. We're going to go see Robin."

"I thought Robin died," I said.

Pat made a face. "Yes, well," she said.

"That hospital was such a bad scene," said Isabel. She was not wearing her prosthetic arm. Except in pieces choreographed by others, she almost never did anymore. "But she's back home now and she's expecting us."

"How can that be?"

"You know women and their houses," said Pat. "It's hard for them to part company." Pat had had a massive stroke two years before, which had wiped out her ebullient personality and her short-term memory, but periodically her wounded, recovering brain cast about desperately and landed on a switch and threw it, and she woke up in a beautiful manic frenzy, seeming like the old Pat, saying, "I feel like I've been asleep for years," and she would stay like that for days on end, insomniac and babbling and reminiscing, painting her paintings, then she'd crash again, passive and mute. She was on disability leave and had a student living with her full-time who took care of her.

"Maybe we all drink too much gin," I said.

For a moment there was just silence. "Are you referring to the accident?" said Isabel accusingly. It was a car crash that had severed her arm. A surgeon and his team of residents had sewn it back on, but the arm had bled continually through the skin grafts and was painful—the first dance afterward before an audience, a solo performed with much spinning and swinging from a rope, had flung specks of blood to the stage floor—and after a year, and a small ineffectual codeine habit, she'd gone back to the same surgeon and asked him to remove it, the whole arm, she was done, she had tried.

"No, no," I said. "I'm not referring to anything."

"So hey, come on, come on!" said Pat. The switch seemed to have been thrown in her.

"Robin's waiting."

"What do I bring?"

"Bring?" Pat and Isabel burst out laughing. "You're kidding, right?" Pat said.

"She's kidding," said Isabel. She felt the sleeve of my orange sweater, which I was still wearing. "Hey. This color looks nice on you. Where did you get this?"

"I forget."

"Yeah, so do I!" said Pat, and she and Isabel burst into fits of hilarity again.

I put on shoes, grabbed a jacket, and left with them.

Isabel drove, one-armed, to Robin's. When we arrived the house was completely dark, but the streetlights showed once more the witchy strangeness of the place. Because she wrote plays based on fairy tales, Robin had planted in the yard, rather haphazardly, the trees and shrubs that figured most prominently in the tales: apple, juniper, hazelnut, and rosebushes. Unfortunately, our latitude was not the best gardening zone for these. Even braced and trussed, they had struggled, jagged and leggy; at this time of year, when they were leafless and bent, one couldn't say for sure whether they were even alive. Spring would tell.

Why would a man focus on her garage when there was this crazed landscaping with which to judge her? Make your excuses: no jury would convict.

Though why would a man focus on anything but her?

We parked in the driveway, where Robin's own car was still parked, her garage no doubt locked—even in the dark one could see the boxes stacked against the single garage window that faced the street.

"The key's under the mat," said Isabel, though I didn't know this and wondered how she did. Pat found the key, unlocked the door, and we all went in. "Don't turn on the lights," Isabel added.

"I know," whispered Pat, though *I* didn't know.

"Why can't we turn on the lights?" I asked, also in a whisper. The door closed behind us and we stood there in the quiet, pitch-black house.

"The police," said Pat.

"No, not the police," said Isabel.

"Then what?"

"Never mind. Just give it a minute and our eyes will adjust." We stood there listening to our own breathing. We didn't move, so as not to trip over anything.

And then on the opposite side of the room a small light flicked on from somewhere at the end of the far hallway; we could not see down it, but out stepped Robin, looking pretty much the same, though she had a white cotton scarf wrapped and knotted around her neck. Against the white, her teeth had a fluorescent ocher sheen, but otherwise she looked regal and appraising, and she smiled at all of us, including me—though more tentatively, I thought, at me. Then she put her finger to her lips and shook her head, so we didn't speak. She walked toward us.

"You came" were her first hushed words, directed at me. "I missed you a little at the hospital." Her smile had become clearly tight and judging.

"I am so sorry," I said.

"That's OK, they'll tell you," she said, indicating Is and Pat. "It was a little nuts."

"It was totally nuts," said Pat.

"As a result?" whispered Robin. "No hugs. Everything's a little precarious, between the postmortem and the tubes in and out all week. This scarf's the only thing holding my head on." Though she was pale, her posture was perfect, her dark red hair restored, her long thin arms folded across her chest. She was dressed as she always dressed: in black jeans and a blue sweater. She simply, newly, had the imperial standoffishness I realized only then that I had always associated with the dead. We pulled up chairs and then each of us sat.

"Should we make some gin rickeys?" Isabel asked, motioning toward the bags of booze and lime juice blend.

"We wanted to come here and each present you with something," said Pat.

"We did?" I said. I'd brought nothing. I had asked them what to bring and they had laughed it off.

Robin looked at me. "Always a little out of the loop, eh?" She smiled stiffly.

Pat was digging around in a hemp tote bag I hadn't noticed before. "Here's a little painting I made for you," she said, handing a small unframed canvas gingerly to Robin. I couldn't see what the painting was of. Robin stared at it for a very long time and then looked back up at Pat and said, "Thank you so much." She momentarily laid the painting in her lap and I could see it was nothing but a plain white blank.

I looked longingly at the paper sack of gin.

"And I have a new dance for you!" whispered Isabel excitedly at Robin.

"You do?" I said.

Robin turned to me again. "Always the last to know, huh," she said and then winced, as if speaking hurt. She clutched Pat's painting to her stomach.

Isabel stood and moved her chair out of the way. "This piece is dedicated to Robin Ross," she announced. And then, after a moment's stillness, she began to move, saying lines of poetry as she did. "'Heap not on this mound / Roses that she loved so well; / Why bewilder her with roses / That she cannot see or smell?'" There was more, and as, reciting, she flew and turned and balanced on one leg, her single arm aloft, I thought, *What the hell kind of poem is this?* It seemed rude to speak of death to the dead, and I kept checking in with Robin's face, to see how she was taking it, but Robin remained impassive. At the end, she placed the painting back in her lap and clapped. I was about to clap as well, when car headlights from the driveway suddenly arced across the room.

"It's the cops! Get down!" said Isabel, and we all hit the floor.

"They're patrolling the house," whispered Robin, lying on her back on the rug. She was hugging Pat's painting to her chest. "I guess there have been calls from a neighbor or something. Just lie here for a minute and they'll leave." The police car idled in the driveway for a minute, perhaps taking down the license number of Isabel's car, and then pulled away.

"It's OK. We can get up now," said Robin.

"Whew. That was close," said Pat.

We all got back into our chairs and there was then a long silence, like a Quaker wedding, which I came to understand was being directed at me.

"Well, I guess it's my turn," I said. "It's been a terrible month. First the election, and now this. You." I indicated Robin, and she nodded just slightly, then grabbed at her scarf and retied the knot. "And I don't have my violin or my piano here," I said. Isabel and Pat were staring at me hopelessly. "So—I guess I'll just sing." I stood up and cleared my throat. I knew that if you took "The Star-Spangled Banner" very slowly and mournfully, it altered not just the attitude of the song but the actual punctuation, turning it into a protest and a question. I sang it slowly, not without a little twang. "O say does that star-spangled banner yet wave, o'er the land of the free and the home of the brave?" Then I sat down. The three of them applauded, Isabel slapping her thigh with one hand.

"Very nice," Robin said to me. "You never sing enough," she added, ambiguously. Her smile to me was effortful and pinched. "Now I have to go," she said, and she stood, leaving Pat's painting behind on the chair, and walked into the lit hallway, after which we heard the light switch flick off. The whole house was plunged into darkness again.

"Well, I'm glad we did that," I said on the way back home. I was sitting alone in the back, sneaking some of the gin—why bother ever again with rickey mix?—and I'd been staring out the window. Now I looked forward and noticed that Pat was driving. Pat hadn't driven in years. A pickup truck with the bumper sticker NO HILLARY NO WAY roared past us, and we stared at its message as if we were staring at a swastika. Where were we living?

"Redneck," Isabel muttered at the driver.

"It's a trap, isn't it?" I said.

"What is?" asked Pat.

"This place!" exclaimed Isabel. "Our work! Our houses! The college!"

"It's all a trap!" I repeated.

But we did not entirely believe it. Somewhere inside us we were joyful orphans: our lives were right, we were zooming along doing what we wanted, we were sometimes doing what we loved. But we were inadequate as a pit crew, for ourselves or for anyone else. "It was good to see Robin," I continued from the back. "It was really good to see her."

"That's true," said Isabel. Pat said nothing. She was coming off her manic high and driving took all she had.

"All in all it was a good night," I said.

"A good night," agreed Isabel.

"Good night," Robin had said the last time I'd seen her well, standing in her own doorway. She had invited me over and we had hung out, eating her summery stir-fry, things both lonely and warm between us, when she asked about the man I was seeing, the one she had dated briefly.

"Well, I don't know," I said, a little sad. At that point I was still sitting at her table and I found myself rubbing the grain of it with one finger. "He seems now also to be seeing this other person—Daphne Kern? Do you know her? She's one of those beautician-slash-art dealers?" All the restaurants, coffee shops, and hair salons in town seemed to have suddenly gotten into hanging, showing, and selling art. This dignified, or artified, the business of serving. Did I feel I was better, more interesting, with my piano and my violin and my singing?

"I know Daphne. I took a yoga class once from her, when she was doing that."

"You did?" I could not control myself. "So what's so compelling about her?" My voice was not successfully shy of a whine. "Is she nice?"

"She's pretty, she's nice, she's intuitive," Robin said, casually ticking off the qualities. "She's actually a talented yoga instructor. She's very physical. Even when she speaks she uses her body a lot. You know, frankly? She's probably just really good in bed."

At this my heart sickened and plummeted down my left side and into my shoe. My appetite, too, shrank to a small pebble and sat in stony reserve in the place my heart had been and to which my heart would at some point return, but not in time for dessert.

"I've made a lemon meringue pie," said Robin, getting up and clearing the dishes. She was always making pies. She would have written more plays if she had made fewer pies. "More meringue than lemon, I'm afraid."

"Oh, thank you. I'm just full," I said, looking down at my unfinished food.

"I'm sorry," Robin said, a hint of worry in her voice. "Should I not have said that thing about Daphne?"

"Oh, no," I said. "That's fine. It's nothing." But soon I felt it was time for me to go, and after a single cup of tea, I stood, clearing only a few of the dishes with her. I found my purse and headed for the door.

She stood in the doorway, holding the uneaten meringue pie. "That skirt, by the way, is great," she said in the June night. "Orange is a good color on you. Orange and gold."

"Thanks," I said.

Then, without warning, she suddenly lifted up the pie and pushed it into her own face. When she pulled off the tin, meringue clung to her skin like blown snow. The foam of it covered her lashes and brows, and with her red hair for a minute she looked like a demented Queen Elizabeth.

"What the *fuck*?" I said, shaking my head. I needed new friends. I would go to more conferences and meet more people.

"I've always wanted to do that," said Robin. The mask of meringue on her face looked eerie, not clownish at all, and her mouth speaking through the white foam seemed to be a separate creature entirely, a puppet or a fish. "I've always wanted to do that, and now I have."

"Hey," I said. "There's no business like show business." I was digging in my purse for my car keys.

Long hair flying over her head, bits of meringue dropping on the porch, she took a deep dramatic bow. "Everything," she added, from behind her mask, "everything, everything, well, almost everything about it"—she gulped a little pie that had fallen in from one corner of her mouth—"is appealing."

"Brava," I said, smiling. I had found my keys. "Now I'm out of here."

"Of course," she said, gesturing with her one pie-free hand. "Onward."

for Nietzchka Keene (1952–2004)

PAPER LOSSES

Although Kit and Rafe had met in the peace movement, marching, organizing, making no nukes signs, now they wanted to kill each other. They had become, also, a little pro-nuke. Married for two decades of precious, precious life, she and Rafe seemed currently to be partners only in anger and dislike, their old lusty love mutated to rage. It was both the shame and the demise of them that hate like love could not live on air. And so in this, their newly successful project together, they were complicitous and synergistic. They were nurturing, homeopathic, and enabling. They spawned and raised their hate together, cardiovascularly, spiritually, organically. In tandem, as a system, as a dance team of bad feeling, they had shoved their hate center stage and shown a spotlight down for it to seize. *Do your stuff, baby! Who's the best? Who's the man?*

"Pro-nuke? You are? Really?" Kit was asked by friends, to whom she continued indiscreetly to complain.

"Well, no." Kit sighed. "But in a way."

"You seem like you need someone to talk to."

Which hurt Kit's feelings, since she'd felt she was talking to *them*. "I'm just concerned about the kids," Kit said.

Rafe had changed. His smile was just a careless yawn, or was his smile just stuck carelessly on? Which was the correct lyric? She did not know. But, for sure, he had changed. In Beersboro they put things neutrally, like that. Such changes were couched.

No one ever said a man was now completely screwed up. They said, *The guy has changed.* Rafe had started to make model rockets in the basement. He'd become *a little different.* He was something of *a character.* The brazen might suggest, *He's gotten into some weird shit.* The rockets were tall, plastic, penile-shaped things to which Rafe carefully shellacked authenticating military decals. What had happened to the handsome hippie she had married? He was prickly and remote, empty with fury. A blankness had entered his blue-green eyes. They stayed wide and bright but nonfunctional—like dime-store jewelry. She wondered if this was a nervous breakdown, the genuine article. But it persisted for months and she began to suspect, instead, a brain tumor. Occasionally he catcalled and wolf-whistled across his mute alienation, his pantomime of hate momentarily collapsed. "Hey, cutie," he would call to her from the stairs, after not having looked her in the eye for two months. It was like being snowbound with someone's demented uncle: Should marriage be like that? She wasn't sure.

She seldom saw him anymore when he got up in the morning and left for his office. And when he came home from work, he would disappear down the basement stairs. Nightly, in the anxious conjugal dusk that was now their only life together, after the kids went to bed, the house would fill up with fumes. When she called down to him about this he never answered. He seemed to have turned into some sort of space alien. Of course later she would understand that all this meant he was involved with another woman, but at the time, protecting her own vanity and sanity, she was working with two hypotheses only: brain tumor or space alien.

"All husbands are space aliens," said her friend Jan.

"God help me, I had no idea," said Kit. She began spreading peanut butter on a pretzel and eating quickly.

"In fact," said Jan, "my sister and I call them UFOs."

It stood for something. Kit hated to ask.

"Ungrateful fuckers," Jan said.

Kit thought for a moment. "But what about the *o*?" she asked. "You said *UFO*."

There was a short silence. "Ungrateful fuckeroos," Jan added quickly. "I know that doesn't make perfect sense."

"He's in such disconnect. His judgment is so bad."

"Not on the planet he lives on. On *his* planet he's a veritable Solomon. 'Bring the stinkin' baby to me now!'"

"Do you think people can be rehabilitated and forgiven?"

"Sure! Look at Ollie North."

"Well, he lost that Senate race. He was not sufficiently forgiven."

"But he got some votes," Jan insisted.

"Yeah, and now what is he doing?"

"Now he's back promoting a line of fire-retardant pajamas. It's a life!" Jan paused. "Do you fight about it?"

"About what?" asked Kit.

"The rockets back to his homeland."

Kit sighed. "Yes, the toxic military crafts business poisoning our living space. Do I fight? I don't fight I just, well, OK: I ask a few questions from time to time. I ask, 'What the hell are you doing?' I ask, 'Are you trying to asphyxiate your entire family?' I ask, 'Did you hear me?' Then I ask, 'Did you hear me?' again. Then I ask, 'Are you deaf?' I also ask, 'What do you think a marriage is? I'm really just curious to know,' and also, 'Is this your idea of a well-ventilated place?' A simple interview, really.

I don't believe in fighting. I believe in giving peace a chance. I also believe in internal bleeding." She paused to shift the phone more comfortably against her face. "I'm also interested," Kit said, "in those forensically undetectable dissolving plastic bullets. Have you heard of those?"

"No."

"Well, maybe I'm wrong about those. I'm probably wrong. That's where the Mysterious Car Crash may have to come in." In the chrome of the refrigerator she caught the reflection of her own face, part brunette Shelley Winters, part potato, the finely etched sharps and accidentals beneath her eyes a musical interlude amidst the bloat. In every movie she had seen with Shelley Winters in it, Shelley Winters was the one who died. Peanut butter was stuck high and dry on Kit's gums. On the counter a large old watermelon had begun to sag and pull apart in the middle along the curve of seeds, like a shark's grin, and she lopped off a wedge, rubbed its cool point around the inside of her mouth. It had been a year since Rafe had kissed her. She sort of cared and sort of didn't. A woman had to choose her own particular unhappiness carefully. That was the only happiness in life: to choose the best unhappiness. An unwise move, good God, you could squander everything.

The summons took her by surprise. It came in the mail, addressed to her, and there it was, stapled to divorce papers. She'd been properly served. The bitch had been papered. Like a person, a marriage was unrecognizable in death, even buried in an excellent suit. Atop the papers themselves was a letter from Rafe suggesting their spring wedding anniversary as the final divorce date. *Why not complete the symmetry?* he wrote, which didn't even sound like him, though its heartless efficiency was suited to this, his new life as a space alien, and in keeping generally with the principles of space alien culture. The papers referred to Kit and Rafe by their legal names, Katherine and Raphael, as if it were the more formal versions of themselves who were divorcing—their birth certificates were divorcing!—and not they themselves. Rafe was still living in the house and had not told her yet he'd bought a new one. "Honey," she said trembling, "something very interesting came in the mail today."

Rage had its medicinal purposes, but she was not wired to sustain it, and when it tumbled away, loneliness engulfed her, grief burning at the center in a cold blue heat. At two different funerals of elderly people she hardly knew she went in and wept in the back row of the church like a secret lover of the deceased. She felt woozy and ill and never wanted to see Rafe—or rather, Raphael—again, but they had promised the kids this Caribbean vacation, so what could they do. This at last was what all those high school drama classes had been for: acting. She once had played the queen in *The Winter's Tale* and once a changeling child in a play called *Love Me Right Now,* written by one of the more disturbing English teachers in her high school. In both of these she learned that time was essentially a comic thing—only constraints upon it forced it to tragedy, or at least to misery. Romeo and Juliet, Tristan and Isolde—if only they'd had more time! Marriage stopped being comic when it was suddenly halted, at which point it became divorce, which time never disrupted, and so the funniness of which was never-ending.

Still, Rafe mustered up thirty seconds of utterance in order to persuade her not to join them on this vacation. "I don't think you should go," he announced.

"I'm going," she said.

"We'll be giving the children false hope."

"Hope is never false. Or it's always false. Whatever. It's just hope," she said. "Nothing wrong with that."

"I just don't think you should go." Divorce, she could see, would be like marriage: a power grab, as in who would be the dog and who would be the owner of the dog?

What bimbo did he want to give her ticket to? (Only later would she find out. "As a feminist you mustn't blame the other woman," a neighbor told her. "As a feminist I request that you no longer speak to me," Kit replied.)

And months later, in the courtroom, where she would discover that the county owned her marriage and that the county was now taking it back like a chicken franchise she had made a muck of, forbidding her to own another franchise for six more months, with the implication that she might want to stay clear of all poultry cuisine for a much longer time than that, when she had finally to pronounce in front of the robed, robotic judge and a winking stenographer whose winking seemed designed to keep the wives from crying, she would have to declare the marriage "irretrievably broken." What second-rate poet had gotten hold of the divorce laws? She would find the words sticking in her throat, untrue in their conviction. Was not everything fixable? This age of disposables, was it not also an age of fantastic adhesives? Why "irretrievably broken" like a songbird's wing? Why not "Do you find this person you were married to, and who is now sitting next to you in the courtroom, a total asshole?" That would suffice, and be more accurate. The term "irretrievably broken" sent one off into an eternity of wondering. Whereas the other did not.

———

She and Rafe had not yet, however, signed the papers. And there was the matter of her wedding ring, which was studded with little junk emeralds and which she liked a lot and hoped she could continue wearing because it didn't look like a typical wedding ring. He had removed his ring—which did look like a typical wedding ring—a year earlier because he said it "bothered" him. She had thought at the time he'd meant it was rubbing. He had often just shed his clothes spontaneously—when they had first met he was something of a nudist. It was good to date a nudist: things moved right along. But it was not good trying to stay married to one. Soon she would be going on chaste geriatric dates with other people whose clothes would, like hers, remain glued to the body.

"What if I can't get my ring off," she said to him now on the plane to La Caribe, the gringo enclave Rafe had chosen. She had gained a little weight in their twenty years of marriage but really not all *that* much. She had been practically a child bride! "Send me the sawyer's bill," he said. Oh, the sparkle in his eye *was* gone!

"What is wrong with you?" she said. Of course, she blamed his parents, who had somehow, long ago, accidentally or on purpose, raised him as a space alien, with space alien values, space alien thoughts, and the hollow shifty character, concocted guilelessness, and sociopathic secrets of a space alien.

"What is wrong with *you*?" he snarled. This was his habit, his space alien habit, of merely repeating what she had just said to him. It had to do, no doubt, with his central nervous system, a silicon-chipped information processor incessantly encountering new linguistic combinations, which it then had to absorb and file. Repetition bought time and assisted the storage process.

More than the girls, who were just little, she was worried
about Sam, their sensitive fourth grader, who now sat across
the airplane aisle moodily staring out the window at the clouds.
Soon, through the machinations of the extremely progressive
divorce laws—a boy needs his dad!—she would no longer see
him every day; he would become a boy who no longer saw his
mother every day, and he would scuttle and float a little off and
away like paper carried by wind. With time he would harden:
he would eye her over his glasses, in the manner of a maître d'
suspecting the arrival of riffraff. But on this, their last trip as
an actual family, he did fairly well at not letting on. They all
slept in the same room, in separate beds, and saw other families squalling and squabbling, so that by comparison theirs—
a family about to break apart forever—didn't look so bad. She
was not deceived by the equatorial sea breeze and so did not
overbake herself in the colonial sun; with the resort managers
she shared her moral outrage at the armed guards who kept the
local children from sneaking past the fence onto this white,
white beach; and she rubbed a kind of resin into her brow to
freeze it there and downplay the creases—to appear younger
for her departing husband, though he never once looked at
her. Not that she looked that good: her suitcase had gotten
lost and she was forced to wear clothes purchased from the
gift shop—the words LA CARIBE emblazoned across every single
thing.

On the beach people read books about Rwandan and Yugo-
slavian genocide. This was to add seriousness to a trip that
lacked it. One was supposed not to notice the dark island
boys on the other side of the guards and barbed wire, throwing rocks. When a cruise ship temporarily docked in the bay,

and then departed, she joined some other tourists on the beach to shout at the boat, "Don't let the door hit you in the ass!" as if they were different and not all of them tourists, seeking to console themselves with hierarchies of tourism, to keep the stone-throwing boys from one's thoughts.

There were ways of making things temporarily vanish. One could disappear oneself in movement and repetition. Sam liked only the trampoline and nothing else. There were dolphin rides, but Sam sensed their cruelty. "They speak a language," he said. "We shouldn't ride them."

"They look happy," said Kit.

Sam looked at her with seriousness from some sweet beyond. "They look happy so you won't kill them."

"You think so?"

"If dolphins tasted good," he said, "we wouldn't even know about their language." That the intelligence in a thing could undermine your appetite for it. That yumminess obscured the mind of the yummy as well as the mind of the yummer. That deliciousness resulted in decapitation. That you could only understand something if you did not desire it. How did he know these things already? Usually girls realized this first. But not hers. Her girls, Beth and Dale, were tough beyond Kit's comprehension: practical, self-indulgent, independent five-year-old twins, a system unto themselves. They had their own secret world of Montessori code words and plastic jewelry and spells of hilarity brought on mostly by the phrase "cinnamon M&M's" repeated six times fast. They wore sparkly fairy wings wherever they went, even over cardigans, and they car-

ried wands. "I'm a big brother now," Sam had said repeatedly
to everyone and with uncertain pride the day the girls were
born, and after that he spoke not another word on the matter. Sometimes, silently, Kit accidentally referred to Beth and
Dale as Death and Bail, as they buried their several Barbies in
sand, then lifted them out again with glee. Anyone near, on a
towel, reading of holocausts, turned and smiled. In this fine, far
compound on the sea, the contradictions of life were grotesque
and uninventable. She went to the central office and signed up
for a hot stone massage: "Would you like a man or a woman?"
asked the receptionist.

"Excuse me?" asked Kit, stalling—after all these years of
marriage, which *did* she want? What did she know of *men*—or
women? "There's no such thing as *men*," her friend Jan used to
say, until recently. "Every man is different. The only thing they
have in common is—well—a capacity for horrifying violence."

"A man or a woman—for the massage?" Kit asked now, buy-
ing time. She thought of the slow mating of snails, an entire
day, being hermaphrodites and having it all be so confusing: by
the time they had it figured out who was going to be the girl
and who was going to be the boy someone came along with
some garlic paste and just swooped them right up.

"Oh, either one," she said, and then she knew she'd get a
man. Whom she tried not to look at but could smell in all
his smoky aromas—tobacco, incense, cannabis—exhaling and
swirling their way around him. A wiry old American pothead
gone to grim seed, he had the Dickensian name of Daniel Han-
dler, and he did not speak. He placed hot stones along her back
and left them there in a line up her spine—did she think her
belotioned flesh too private and precious to be touched by the

likes of him? Are you *crazy*? The mad joy pulsing in her face was held over the floor by the table headpiece and at his touch her eyes filled with bittersweet tears, which then dripped out her nose, which she realized then was positioned perfectly by God as a little drainpipe for crying. The sad massage hut carpet beneath her grew a spot. He left the hot stones on her until they went cold. As each one lost its heat she could no longer feel it even there on her back, and then its removal was like a discovery that it had been there all along: how strange to forget and feel it only then, at the end; though this wasn't the same thing as the frog in the pot whose water slowly heats and boils, still it had meaning, she felt, the way metaphors of a thermal nature tended to. Then he took all the stones off and pressed the hard edges of them deep into her back, between the bones, in a way that felt mean—perhaps in embittered rage about his own life—but that more likely had no intention at all. "That was nice," she said at the end, when she saw him putting all his stones away. He had heated them in a plastic electric Crock-Pot filled with water, she saw, and now he unplugged the thing in a tired fashion.

"Where did you get those stones?" she asked. They were smooth and dark gray—black when wet, she could see.

"They're river stones," he said. "I've been collecting them for years up in Colorado." He replaced them in a metal fishing tackle box.

"You live in Colorado?" she asked.

"Used to," he said, and that was that. Later that day they would see each other at the Farmacia de Jesus and look the other way.

Kit got dressed. "Someday you, like me, will have done sufficient lab work," Jan had said. "Soon you, like me, in your next life, like me, will want them old and rich, on their deathbed, really, and with no sudden rallyings in the hospice."

"You're a woman of steel and ice," Kit had said.

"Not at all," Jan had said. "I'm just a voice on the phone, drinking a little tea."

On their last night of vacation Kit's suitcase arrived like a joke. She didn't even open it. They put out the paper doorknob flag that said WAKE US UP FOR THE SEA TURTLES. The doorknob flag had a preprinted request to be woken at 3:00 a.m. so that they could go to the beach and see the hatching of the baby sea turtles and their quick scuttle into the ocean, under the cover of night, to avoid predators. But though Sam had hung the flag carefully and before the midnight deadline, no staffperson awoke them. And by the time they got up and went down to the beach it was ten in the morning. Strangely, the sea turtles were still there. They had hatched in the night and then hotel personnel had hung on to them, in a baskety cage, to show them off to the tourists who'd been too lazy or deaf to have gotten up in time. "Look, come see!" said a man with a Spanish accent who usually rented out the scuba gear. Sam, Beth, Dale, Kit all ran over. (Rafe stayed behind to drink coffee and read the paper.) The squirming babies were beginning to heat up in the warming sun; the goldening Venetian vellum of their wee webbed feet was already edged in dessicating brown. "I'm going to have to let them go now," said the man. "You are the last ones to see these little *bebés*." He took them over to the water's edge and let them go, hours too late, to make their own way into the sea. And one by one a frigate bird swooped in, plucked them from the silver waves, and ate them for breakfast.

Kit sank down in a large chair next to Rafe. He was tanning himself, she could see, for someone else's lust. "I think I need a drink," she said. The kids were swimming.

"Don't expect me to buy you a drink," he said.

Had she even asked? Did she now call him the bitterest name she could think of? Did she stand and turn and slap him across the face in front of several passersby? Who told you *that*?

When they left La Caribe, its crab claws of land extending into the blue bay, she was glad. Staying there she had begun to hate the world. In the airports and on the planes home, she did not even try to act natural: natural was a felony. She spoke to her children calmly, from a script, with dialogue and stage directions of utter neutrality. Back home in Beersboro she unpacked the condoms and candles, her little love sack, completely unused, and threw it all in the trash. What had she been thinking? Later, when she had learned to tell this story differently, as a story, she would construct a final lovemaking scene of sentimental vengeance that would contain the inviolable center of their love, the sweet animal safety of night after night, the still-beating tender heart of marriage. But for now she would become like her unruinable daughters, and even her son, who as he aged stoically and carried on regardless would come scarcely to recall—was it past even imagining?—that she and Rafe had ever been together at all.

FOES

Bake McKurty was no stranger to the parasitic mixings of art and commerce, literature and the rich. "Hedge funds and haiku!" he'd exclaimed to his wife, Suzy—and yet such mixings seemed never to lose their swift, stark capacity to appall. The hustle for money met the hustle for virtue and everyone washed their hands in one another. It was a common enough thing, though was there ever enough soap to cut the grease? "That's what your lemon is for," Suzy would say, pointing at the twist in the martini he was not supposed to drink. Still, now and again, looking up between the crabmeat cocktail and the palate-cleansing sorbet sprinkled with fennel pollen dust, he felt shocked by the whole thing.

"It's symbiosis," said Suzy as they were getting dressed to go. "Think of it being like the krill that grooms and sees for the rock shrimp. Or that bird who picks out the bugs from the rhino hide."

"So we're the Seeing Eye krill," he said.

"Yes!"

"We're the oxpeckers."

"Well, I wasn't going to say that," she said.

"A lot in this world has to do with bugs," said Bake.

"Food," she said. "A lot has to do with grooming and food. Are you wearing that?"

"What's wrong with it?"

"Lose the— What are those?"

"Suspenders."

"They're red."

"OK, OK. But you know, I never do that to you."

"I'm the sighted krill," she said. She smoothed his hair, which had recently become a weird pom-pom of silver and maize.

"And I'm the blind boy?"

"Well, I wasn't going to say that either."

"You look good. Whatever it is your wearing. See? I say nice things to *you*!"

"It's a sarong." She tugged it up a little.

He ripped off the suspenders. "Well, here. You may need these."

They were staying at a Georgetown B and B to save a little money, a town house where the owner-couple left warm cookies at everyone's door at night to compensate for their loud toddler, who by 6:00 a.m. was barking orders and pointing at her mother to fetch this toy or that. After a day of sightseeing—all those museums prepaid with income taxes; it was like being philanthropists come to investigate the look of their own money—Suzy and Bake were already tired. They hailed a cab and recited the address of the event to the cabbie, who nodded and said ominously, "Oh, yes."

Never mind good taste, here at this gala even the usual diaphanous veneer of seemliness had been tossed to the trade winds: the fund-raiser for *Lunar Lines Literary Journal*—3LJ as it was known to its readers and contributors; "the magazine" as it was known to its staff, as if there were no others—was being held in a bank. Or at least a former bank, one which had recently gone under, and which now sold squid-ink orecchiette beneath its vaulted ceilings, and martinis and grenache from its former teller stations. Wood and marble were preserved and buffed, glass barriers removed. In the evening light the place was golden. It was cute! So what if subtle boundaries of occasion and transaction had been given up on? So what if this were a mausoleum of greed now danced in by all? He and Suzy had been invited. The passive voice could always be used to obscure blame.

The invitation, however, to this D.C. fund-raiser seemed to Bake a bit of a fluke, since *Man on a Quarter, Man on a Horse,* Bake's ill-selling biography of George Washington (in a year when everyone was obsessed with Lincoln, even the efficiently conflated Presidents' Day had failed to help his book sales), would appear to fit him to neither category of guest. But *Lunar Lines,* whose offices were in Washington, had excerpted a portion of it, as if in celebration of their town. And so Bake was sent two free dinner tickets. He would have to rub elbows and charm the other guests—the rich, the magazine's donors, who would be paying five hundred dollars a plate. Could he manage that? Could he be the court jester, the town clown, the token writer at the table? "Absolutely," he lied.

Why had he come? Though it was named after the man he had devoted years of affectionate thought and research to, he had never liked this city. An ostentatious company town built on a marsh—a mammoth, pompous chit-ridden motor vehicle department run by gladiators. High-level clerks on the take, their heads full of unsound sound bites and falsified recall. "Yes! How are you? It's been a while." Not even "It's been a long time," because who knew? Perhaps it hadn't been. Better just to say, neutrally, "It's been a while," and no one could argue.

He clung to Suzy. "At least the wine is good," she said. They weren't really mingling. They were doing something that was more like a stiff list, a drift and sway. The acoustics made it impossible to speak normally, and so they found themselves shouting inanities, then just falling mute. The noise of the place was deafening as a sea, and the booming heartiness of others seemed to drown all possibility of happiness for themselves.

"Soon we'll have to find our table," he shouted, glancing out at the vast room filled with a hundred white-clothed circles, flickering with candlelight. Small vases of heather sprigs that could easily catch fire had been placed in the centers as well. So were little chrome cardholders declaring the table numbers. "What number are we?"

Suzy pulled the tag from what he facetiously called her "darling little bag," then shoved it back in. "Seventy-nine," she said. "I hope that's near the restroom."

"I hope it's near the exit."

"Let's make a dash for it now!"

"Let's scream 'fire!'"

"Let's fake heart attacks!"

"Do you have any pot?"

"We flew here—remember? I wouldn't bring pot on an airplane."

"We're losing our sense of adventure. In all things."

"This is an adventure!"

"You see, that's what I mean."

At the ringing of a small bell everyone was to sit—not just

the ones already in wheelchairs. Bake let Suzy lead as they wended their way, drinks in hand, between the dozens of tables that were between them and number 79. They were the first ones there, and when he looked at the place cards and saw that someone had placed Suzy far away from him, he quickly switched the seating arrangements and placed her next to him, on his left. "I didn't come this far not to sit next to you," he said, and she smiled wanly, squeezing his hand. These kinds of gestures were necessary, since they had not had sex in six months. "I'm sixty and I'm on antidepressants," Bake had said when Suzy had once (why only once?) complained. "I'm lucky my penis hasn't dropped off."

They remained standing by their seats, waiting for their table to fill up: Soon a young investor couple from Wall Street who had not yet lost their jobs. Then a sculptor and her son. Then an editorial assistant from 3LJ. Then last, to claim the seat to his right, a brisk young Asian woman in tapping heels. She thrust her hand out to greet him. Her nails were long and painted white—perhaps they were fake: Suzy would know, though Suzy was now sitting down and talking to the sculptor next to her.

"I'm Linda Santo," the woman to his right said, smiling. Her hair was black and shiny and long enough so that with a toss of the head she could swing it back behind her shoulder and short enough that it would fall quickly forward again. She was wearing a navy blue satin dress and a string of pearls. The red shawl she had wrapped over her shoulders she now placed on the back of her seat. He felt a small stirring in him. He had always been attracted to Asian women, though he knew he mustn't ever mention this to Suzy, or to anyone really.

"I'm Baker McKurty," he said, shaking her hand.

"Baker?" she repeated.

"I usually go by Bake." He accidentally gave her a wink. One had to be very stable to wink at a person and not frighten them.

"Bake?" She looked a little horrified—if one could be horrified only a little. She was somehow aghast—and so he pulled out her chair to show her that he was harmless. No sooner were they all seated than appetizers zoomed in. Tomatoes stuffed with avocados and avocados with tomatoes. It was a witticism—with a Christmasy look though Christmas was a long way away.

"So where are all the writers?" Linda Santo asked him while looking over both her shoulders. The shiny hair flew. "I was told there would be writers here."

"You're not a writer?"

"No, I'm an evil lobbyist," she said, grinning slightly. "Are you a writer?"

"In a manner of speaking, I suppose," he said.

"You are?" She brightened. "What might you have written?"

"What might I have written? Or, what did I actually write?"

"Either one."

He cleared his throat. "I've written several biographies. Boy George. King George. And now George Washington. That's my most recent. A biography of George Washington. A captivating man, really, with a tremendous knack for real estate. And a peevishness about being overlooked for promotion when he served in the British army. The things that will start a war! And I'm not like his other biographers. I don't rule out his being gay."

"You're a biographer of Georges," she said, nodding and unmoved. Clearly she'd been hoping for Don DeLillo.

This provoked him. He veered off into a demented heat. "Actually, I've won the Nobel Prize."

"Really?"

"Yes! But, well, I won it during a year when the media weren't paying a lot of attention. So it kind of got lost in the shuffle. I won—right after 9/11. In the shadow of 9/11. Actually, I won right as the second tower was being hit."

She scowled. "The Nobel Prize for Literature?"

"Oh, for literature? No, no, no—not for literature." His penis now sat soft as a shrinking peach in his pants.

Suzy leaned in on his left and spoke across Bake's plate to Linda. "Is he bothering you? If he bothers you, just let me know. I'm Suzy." She pulled her hand out of her lap, and the two women shook hands over his avocado. He could see Linda's nails were fake. Or, if not fake, something. They resembled talons.

"This is Linda," said Bake. "She's an evil lobbyist."

"Really!" Suzy said good-naturedly, but soon the sculptor was tapping her on the arm and she had to turn back and be introduced to the sculptor's son.

"Is it hard being a lobbyist?"

"It's interesting," she said. "It's hard work but interesting."

"That's the best kind."

"Where are you from?"

"Chicago."

"Oh, really," she said, as if he had announced his close connection to Al Capone. Anyone he ever mentioned Chicago to always brought up Capone. Either Capone or the Cubs.

"So you know the presidential candidate for the Democrats?"

"Brocko? Love him! He's the great new thing. He's a writer

himself. I wonder if he's here." Now Baker, as if in mimicry, turned and looked over both of *his* shoulders.

"He's probably out with his terrorist friends," Linda said.

"He has terrorist friends?" Bake himself had a terrorist friend. Midwesterners loved their terrorist friends, who were usually fine and boring citizens still mythically dining out on the sins of long-ago youth. They never actually killed anyone—at least not intentionally. They aged and fattened in the ordinary fashion. They were rehabilitated. They served their time. And, well, if they didn't, because of *infuriating class privilege that allowed them to just go on as if nothing had ever happened*, well, they raised each other's children and got advanced degrees and gave back to society in other ways. He supposed. He didn't really know much about Chicago. He was actually from Michigan, but when going anywhere he always flew out of O'Hare.

"Uh, yeah. That bomber who tried to blow up federal buildings right here in this town."

"When Brocko was a kid? That sixties guy? But Brocko doesn't even like the sixties. He thinks they're so . . . sixties. The sixties took his mother on some wild ride away from him."

"The sixties *made* him, my friend."

Bake looked at her more closely. Now he could see she wasn't Asian. She had simply had some kind of plastic surgery: skin was stretched and draped strangely around her eyes. A botched eye job. A bad face-lift. An acid peel. Whatever it was: Suzy would know exactly.

"Well, he was a young child."

"So he says."

"Is there some dispute about his age?"

"Where is his birth certificate?"

"I have no idea," said Bake. "I have no idea where my own is."

"Here is my real problem: this country was founded by and continues to be held together by people who have worked very hard to get where they are."

Bake shrugged and wagged his head around. Now would not be the time to speak of timing. It would be unlucky to speak of luck. Could he speak of people having things they didn't deserve, in a roomful of such people? She continued. "And if you don't understand *that*, my friend, then we cannot continue this conversation."

The sudden way in which the whole possibility of communication was now on the line startled him. "I see you've researched the founding of this country." He would look for common ground.

"I watched *John Adams* on HBO. Every single episode."

"Wasn't the guy who played George Washington uncanny? I did think Jefferson looked distractingly like Martin Amis. I wonder if Martin is here?" He looked over his shoulders again. He needed Martin Amis to get over here right now and *help* him.

Linda looked at him fiercely. "It was a great miniseries and a great reminder of the founding principles of our nation."

"Did you know George Washington was afraid of being buried alive?"

"I didn't know about that."

"The guy scarcely had a fear except for that one. You knew he freed his slaves?"

"Hmmmm."

She was eating; he was not. This would not work to his advantage. Nonetheless he went on. "Talk about people who've toiled hard in this country—and yet, not to argue with your thesis too much, those slaves didn't all get ahead."

"Your man Barama, my friend, would not even be in the running if he wasn't black."

Now all appetite left him entirely. The food on his plate, whatever it was, splotches of taupe, dollops of orange, went abstract like a painting. His blood pressure flew up; he could feel the pulsing twitch in his temple. "You know, I never thought about it before but you're right! Being black really *is* the fastest, easiest way to get to the White House!"

She said nothing, and so he added, "Unless you're going by cab, and then, well, it can slow you down a little."

Chewing, Linda looked at him, a flash in her eyes. She swallowed. "Well, supposedly we've already had a black president."

"We have?"

"Yes! A Nobel Prize–winning author said so!"

"Hey. Take it firsthand from me: don't believe everything that a Nobel Prize winner tells you. I don't think a black president ever gets to become president when his nightclub-singer mistress is holding press conferences during the campaign. That would be—that would be a *white* president. Please pass the salt."

The shaker appeared before him. He shook some salt around on his plate and stared at it.

Linda made a stern, effortful smile, struggling to cut something with her knife. Was it meat? Was it poultry? It was consoling to think that, for a change, the rich had had to pay a pretty penny for their chicken while his was free. But it was not consoling *enough*. "If you don't think I as a woman know a thing or two about prejudice, you would be sadly mistaken," Linda said.

"Hey, it's not that easy being a man, either," said Bake. "There's all that cash you have to spend on porn, and believe me, that's money you never get back."

He then retreated, turned toward his left, toward Suzy, and leaned in. "Help me," he whispered in her ear.

"Are you charming the patrons?"

"I fear some object may be thrown."

"You're supposed to charm the patrons."

"I know, I know, I was trying to. I swear. But she's one of those who keeps referring to Brocko as Barama." He had violated most of Suzy's dinner talk rules already: no politics, no religion, no portfolio tips. *And unless you see the head crowning, never look at a woman's stomach and ask if she's pregnant.* He had learned all these the hard way.

But in a year like this one, there was no staying away from certain topics.

"Get back there," Suzy said. The sculptor was tapping Suzy on the arm again.

He tried once more with Linda Santo the evil lobbyist. "Here's the way I see it—and this I think you'll appreciate. It would be great at long last to have a president in the White House whose last name ends with a vowel."

"We've never had a president whose last name ended with a vowel?"

"Well, I don't count Coolidge."

"You're from what part of Chicago?"

"Well, just outside Chicago."

"Where outside?"

"Michigan."

"Isn't Michigan a long way from Chicago?"

"It is!" He could feel the cold air on the skin between his socks and his pant cuffs. When he looked at her hands they seemed frozen into claws.

"People talk about the rock-solid sweetness of the heartland, but I have to say: Chicago seems like a city that has taken too much pride in its own criminal activity." She smiled grimly.

"I don't think that's true." Or was it? He was trying to give her a chance. What if she was right? "Perhaps we have an unfulfilled streak of mythic hankering. Or perhaps we don't live as fearfully as people do elsewhere," he said. Now he was just guessing.

"You wait, my friend, there are some diabolical people eyeing that Sears Tower as we speak."

Now he was silent.

"And if you're in it when it happens, which I hope you're not, but if you are, if you are, if you are, if you're eating lunch at the top or having a meeting down below or whatever it is you may be doing, you will be changed. Because I've been there. I know what it's like to be bombed by terrorists—I was in the Pentagon when they crashed that plane right down into it and I'll tell you: I was burned alive but not dead. I was burned *alive*. It lit me inside. Because of that I know more than ever what this country is about, my friend."

He saw now that her fingernails really were plastic, that the hand really was a dry frozen claw, that the face that had seemed intriguingly exotic had actually been scarred by fire and only partially repaired. He saw how she was cloaked in a courageous and intense hideosity. The hair was beautiful, but now he imagined it was probably a wig. Pity poured through him: he'd never before felt so sorry for someone. How could someone have suffered so much? How could someone have come so close to death, so unfairly, so painfully and heroically, and how could he still want to strangle them?

"You were a lobbyist for the Pentagon?" was all he managed to say.

"Any faux pas?" asked Suzy in the cab on the way back to the B and B, where warm cookies would await them by their door, and snore strips on their nightstand.

"Beaucoup faux," said Bake. He pronounced it *foze*. "Beaucoup verboten foze. Uttering my very name was like standing on the table and peeing in a wineglass."

"What? Oh, please."

"I'm afraid I spoke about politics. I couldn't control myself."

"Brocko is going to win. His daughters will like it here. All will be well. Rest assured," she said, as the cab sped along toward Georgetown, the street curbs rusted and rouged with the first fallen leaves.

"Promise?"

"Promise."

He was afraid to say more.

He did not know how much time he and Suzy might even have left together, and an endgame of geriatric speed dating—everyone deaf and looking identical: "What? I can't hear you? What? You again? Didn't I just see you?"—all taking place midst bankruptcy and war, might be the real circle of hell he was destined for.

"Don't ever leave me," he said.

"Why on earth would I do that?"

He paused. "I'm putting in a request not just for *on earth,* but for even after that."

"OK," she said, and squeezed his meaty thigh. At least he had once liked to think of it as meaty.

"I fear you will soon discover some completely obvious way to find me less than adequate."

"You're adequate," she said.

"I'm adequate enough."

She kept her hand there on his leg, and on top of hers she placed his, the one with the wedding ring she had given him, identical to her own. He willed all his love into the very ends of his fingertips, and as his hand clasped hers he watched the firm, deliberate hydraulics of its knuckles and joints. But she had already turned her head away and was looking out the window, steadily, the rest of the ride back, showing him only her beautiful hair, which was gold and flashing in the passing streetlamps, as if it were something not attached to her at all.

WINGS

Should he find he couldn't work it there would still be
time enough.
                              —Henry James, *The Wings of the Dove*

The grumblings of their stomachs were intertwined and un-
assignable.

"Was that you or was that me?" she would ask in bed, and
Dench would say, "I'm not sure." They lay there in the mornings, their legs moving at angles toward one another, not unlike
the elms she could see through the window outside, the high
branches nuzzling in the late March breeze, speaking tree to
tree of the thrilling weather. Her dreams of eating meals full
of meat, which caused her teeth to gnash in the night—surely
a sign of spring—left the insides of her cheeks bloody and
chewed, one saliva gland now swelled to the size of a raisin.

Shouldn't they be up and about already? Morning sun shot
across the ceiling in a white stripe of paint. She and Dench
were both too young and too old for this close, late-morning,
bed-bound life, but their scuttled careers—the band, the two
CDs, the newsletter (turned e-letter turned abandoned cyber-
litter) on how to simplify your life *(be broke!)*, the driving, the
touring, the scrambling, the foraging in parks for chives and
dandelions, the charging up of credit cards, the taking pictures
of clothes and selling them on eBay ("Wake up!" she used to

exclaim to him in the middle of the night, sitting up in bed, "wake up and listen to my *ideas*!")—had led them here, to a nine-month sublet that allowed pets. Still in their thirties, but barely, they had bought themselves a little time. So what if her investments these days were in pennies, wine corks, and sheets of self-adhesive Forever stamps? These would go up in value, unlike everything else. Beneath her bed was a shoe box of dwindling cash from their last gig, where they'd gotten only a quarter of the door. She could always cut her long, almost Asian hair again, as she had two years ago, and sell it for a thousand dollars.

Now, as she often did when contemplating wrong turns, she sometimes thought back to when it was she had first laid eyes on Dench, that Friday long ago when he had approached her at an afternoon sound check in some downtown or other, his undulating tresses not product-free, a demeanor of arrangement and premeditation that gussied up something more chaotic. Although it was winter he wore mirrored sunglasses and a thin leather jacket with the collar turned up: 150 percent jerk. Perhaps it was his strategy to improve people's opinions of him right away, to catch an upward momentum and make it sail, so when the sunglasses came off and then the jacket, and he began to play a song he had not written himself, he was on his way. He lunged onto one knee and raced through a bludgeoning bass solo. At the drums he pressed the stick into the cymbal and circled it, making a high-pitched celestial note, like a finger going round the edge of a wineglass. He smacked the tambourine against his head and against the snare, back and forth. When he then approached the piano, she stopped him. "Not the piano," she said quietly. "The piano's mine."

"OK," he said. "I just wanted to show you everything I can do." And he picked up an acoustic guitar.

Would it be impossible not to love him? Would not wisdom intervene?

Later, to the rest of the band, whose skepticism toward Dench was edged with polite dismay, she said, "I don't understand why the phrase 'like an orchestra tuning up' is considered a criticism. I love an orchestra when it is tuning up. *Especially* then."

From the beginning, however, she could not see how Dench had ever earned a living. He knew two Ryan Adams songs and played guitar fairly well. But he had never done so professionally. Or done anything professionally that she could discern. Early on he claimed to be waiting for money, and she wasn't sure, when he smiled, whether this was a joke. "From whom? Your mother?" and he only smiled. Which made her think, *Yes indeed, his mother.*

But no. His mother had died when he was a teenager. His father had disappeared years before that and thereafter for Dench there was much moving with his sisters: from Ohio to Indiana to California and back. First with his mom, then with an aunt. There was apparently in his life a lot of dropping in and out of college and unexplained years. There had been a foreshortened stint in the Peace Corps. In Swaziland. "I'd just be waiting at a village bus stop, reading a book, and women would pretend to want to borrow it to read but in truth they just wanted a few pages for toilet paper. Or the guys they had me working with? They would stick their hands in the Port-a-Potties, as soon as we got them off the trucks: they wanted the fragrant blue palms. I had to get out of there, man, I didn't really understand the commitment I had made, and so my uncle got a congressman to pull some strings." How did Dench pay his bills?

"It's one big magic trick," he said. He liked to get high before dinner and seemed never without a joint in his wallet or in a drawer. He ate his chicken—the wings and the drumsticks, the arms and the legs—clean down to the purple bones.

And so, though she could not tell an avocado plant from flax (he had both), and though she had never seen any grow lights or seeds or a framed license to grow medical marijuana from the state of Michigan, KC began to fear Dench made his living by selling pot. It seemed to be the thing he was musing about and not saying. As she had continued to see him, she suspected it more deeply. He played her more songs. Then as something caught fire between them, and love secured its footing inside her, when she awoke next to him with damp knots in the back of her hair like she'd never experienced before, the room full of the previous night's candles and the whiff of weed, his skin beside her a silky calico of cool and warm, and as they both needed to eat and eat some more together, she began to feel OK that he sold drugs. If he did. What the hell? At least there was that. At least he did something. His sleepy smiles and the occasional flash of a euro or a hundred-dollar bill in his pocket seemed to confirm it, but then his intermittent lack of cash altogether perpetuated the mystery, as did his checks, which read D. ENCHER, and she started to fear he might not sell drugs after all. When she asked him straight out, he said only, "You're funny!" And after she had paid for too many of his drinks and meals, since he said he was strapped that week and then the week after that, she began to wish, a little sheepishly, that he did sell drugs. She began to hope deeply that he did. Once she even prayed for him to do so. And soon she was close to begging. *Just a little skunk, darling. Just a little pocket rocket, some sparky bark or kick stick, just a bit of wake and bake . . .*

Instead he joined her band.

It had been called Villa and in the end it had not worked out: tours they paid for themselves with small business loans; audiences who did not like KC's own songs (too singer-songwriter, with rhymes (*calories* and *galleries!*) that she was foolishly proud of (*dead* and *wed!*)), including one tune she refused to part with, since it had briefly been positioned to be a minor indie hit, a song about a chef in New Jersey named Jim Barber whom she'd once been in love with.

Here I am your unshaved fennel
Here I am your unshaved cheese
All I want to know? is when I'll—
feel your blade against my knees.

Its terribleness eluded her. Her lyrics weren't sly or hip or smoky and tough but the demure and simple hopes of a mouse. She'd spent a decade barking up the wrong tree—as a mouse! Audiences booed—the boys in their red-framed spectacles, the girls in their crooked little dresses. Despised especially were her hip-hop renditions of Billy Joel and Neil Young (she was once asked to please sing down by the river, and she'd thought they'd meant the song. She told this sad joke over and over). Throughout the band tours she would wake up weeping at the edge of some bed or other, not knowing where she was or what she was supposed to do that day or once or twice even *who* she was, since all her endeavor seemed separate from herself, a suit to slip into. Tears, she had once been told, were designed to eliminate toxins, and they poured down her face and slimed her neck and gathered in the recesses of her collarbones and she had to be careful never to lie back and let them get into her ears, which might cause the toxins to return and start over. Of course, the rumor of toxins turned out not to be true. Tears were quite pure. And so the reason for them, it seemed to her later, when she thought about it, was to identify the weak, so that the world could assure its strong future by beating the weak to death.

"Are we perhaps unlovable?" she asked Dench.

"It's because we're not named, like, Birth Hearse for Dog-Face."

"Why aren't we named that?"

"Because we have standards."

"Is that it?" she said.

"Yeah! And not just 'Body and Soul' as an encore, though we do that well. I mean we maintain a kind of integrity."

"Integrity! Really!" After too many stolen meals from minibars, the Pringles can carefully emptied and the foil top resealed, the container replaced as if untouched back atop the wood tray, hotel towels along with the gear all packed up in the rental truck whose rear fender bore one large bumper sticker, with Donald Rumsfeld's visage, under which read DOES THIS ASS MAKE MY TRUCK LOOK BIG?, after all that she continually found herself thinking, *If only Dench sold drugs!* On hot summer days she would find a high-end supermarket and not only eat the free samples in their tiny white cups but stand before the produce section and wait for the vegetable misters to come on, holding her arms beneath the water in relief. She was showering with the lettuces.

She and Dench had not developed their talents sufficiently nor cared for them properly—or so a booking agent told them.

Dench took offense. "You forget about the prize perplexity, the award angle—they are often looking for people like us: we could win something!" he exclaimed, with Pringles in his teeth.

The gardenia in KC's throat, the flower that was her singing voice—its brown wilt would have to be painstakingly slowed through the years—had already begun its rapid degeneration into simple crocus, then scraggly weed. She'd been given something perfect—youth!—and done imperfect things with it. The moon shone whole then partial in the sky, having its life without her. Sometimes she just chased roughly after a melody—like someone kicking a can down a road. She had not hemmed in her speaking voice, kept it tame and tended so that her singing one could fly. Her speaking voice was the same as her singing one, a roller coaster of various registers, the Myrna Loy–Billie Burke timbre of the Edwardian grandmother who had raised her, a woman who had trained at conservatory but had never had a singing career and practically sang every sentence she uttered: *Katherine? It's time for dinner* went up and down the scale. Only her dying words—*Marry well*—had been flat, the drone of chagrin, a practical warning: life-preserving but with a glimpse of a dark little bunker in a war not yet declared. *Marry well* had been uttered after she begged KC to get a teaching certificate. *Teaching makes interesting people boring, sure,* she had said. *But it also makes boring people interesting. So there's an upside. There always is an upside if you look up.*

Dench's own poor mother wasn't able to leave him—or his

sisters—a dime, though he had always done what she said, even that one year they lived in motels and he obligingly wore the identical nightgown as his sisters so that they might better be mistaken for a single child, to avoid an extra room charge, in case the maid walked in. His young mother had died with breathing tubes hooked right to her wallet, he said, just sucking it all up. Dench made a big comedic *whooshing* sound when he told this part. His father's disappearance, which had come long before, had devastated and haunted her: when they were out for dinner one night his father announced that he had to see a man about a horse, and he excused himself, went to the men's room, and climbed out the window never to return. Dench made a *whooshing* sound for this part of the story as well.

"I can't decide whether that is cowardice or a weird kind of courage," Dench said.

"It's neither," KC replied. "It has nothing to do with either of those things."

Motherless children would always find each other. She had once heard that. They had the misery that wasn't misery but presumed to be so to others. They had the misery that liked company and *was* company. Only sometimes they felt the facts of their motherless lives. They were a long, long way from home. They had theme songs hatched in a spiritual tradition. There was no fondling of the gold coins of memory. The world was their orphanage.

But when they moved in together he hesitated.

"What about my belongings?" he asked.

"It's not like you have a dog who won't get along with mine," she said.

"I have plants."

"But plants are not a dog."

"Oh, I see: you're one of those people who thinks animals are better, more important than plants!"

She studied him, his eyes large with protest or with drugs or with madness. There were too many things to choose from. "Are you serious?" she asked.

"I don't know," he said and turned to unpack his things.

Now she rose to take the dog for his daily walk. She was wearing an old summer dress as a nightgown, but in the mornings it could work as a dress again, if you just tossed a cardigan over it and put on shoes. In this risky manner, she knew, insanity could encroach.

The sublet she and Dench were in now was a nice one, a fluke, a modern, flat-roofed, stone-and-redwood ranch house with a carport in a neighborhood that was not far from the hospital and was therefore full of surgeons and radiologists and their families. The hospital itself was under construction and the cranes bisected the sky. Big-jawed excavators and backhoes worked beneath lights at night. Walking the dog, she once watched as an excavator's mandibled head was released and fell to the ground; the headless neck then leaned down and began to nudge it, as if trying to find out if it might still be alive. Of course there was an operator, but after that it was hard to think of a creature like this as a machine. When a wall was knocked down, and its quiet secrets sent scattering, the lines between things seemed up for grabs.

The person who owned their house was not connected to the hospital. He was an entrepreneur named Ian who had made a bundle in the nineties on some sort of business software and who for long stretches of time lived out of state—in Ibiza, Zihuatanejo, and Portland—in order to avoid the cold. The house came furnished except, strangely, for a bed, which they bought. On their first day they found food in the refrigerator with not even mold but *dust* on it. "I don't know," said Dench. "Look at the closets. This must be what Ian was using. With hooks this strong maybe we don't need a bed. We can just hang ourselves there at night, like bats."

With Dench she knew, in an unspoken way, that she was the one who was supposed to get them to wherever it was they were going. She was supposed to be the GPS lady who, when you stopped for gas, said, "Get back on the highway." She tried to be that voice with Dench: stubborn, unflappable, keeping to the map and not saying what she knew the GPS lady really wanted to say, which was not "Recalculating" but "What in fucking hell are you thinking?"

"It all may look wrong from outer space, which is where a GPS is seeing it from," Dench would say, when proposing alternatives of any sort, large or small, "but on the ground there's a certain logic. Stick with me on this one. You can have all the others."

There were no sidewalks in this wooded part of town. The sap of the stick-bare trees was just stirring after what looked like a fierce fire of a winter. The roadside gullies that would soon warm and sprout joe-pye weed and pea were still just pebble-flecked mud, and KC's dog, Cat, sniffed his way along, feeling the winter's melt, the ground loosening its fertile odor of wakened worms. Overhead the dirt pearl sky of March hung low as a hat brim. The houses were sidled next to marshes and sycamores, and as she walked along the roads occasionally a car would pass, and she would yank on Cat's leash to heel him close. The roads, all named after colleges out east—Dartmouth Drive, Wellesley Way, Sweet Briar Road; where was her alma mater, SUNY New Paltz Street?—were glistening with the flat glossy colors of flattened box turtles who'd made the spring crossing too slowly and were now stuck to the macadam, thin and shiny as magazine ads.

HOSPICE CARE: IT'S NEVER TOO SOON TO CALL read a billboard near the coffee shop in what constituted the neighborhood's commercial roar. Next to it a traffic sign read PASS WITH CARE. Surrealism could not be made up. It was the very electricity of the real. The largest part of the strip was occupied by an out-of-business bookstore whose plate-glass windows were already cloudy with dust. The D was missing from the sign so that it now read BOR ERS. In insolvency, truth: soon the chain would be shipping its entire stock to the latrines of Swaziland.

Cat was a good dog, part corgi, part Lab, and if KC wore her sunglasses into the coffee shop he could pass for a Seeing Eye dog, and she a blind person, so she didn't have to tie him to a parking sign out front.

The coffee shop played Tom Waits and was elegantly equipped with dimpled cup sleeves, real cream, cinnamon sticks, shakers of sugar. KC got in line. "I love this song," the man in front turned to say to her. He was holding a toddler, and was one of those new urban dads so old he looked like the kidnapper of his own child.

She didn't know what she felt about Tom Waits anymore: his voice had gotten so *industrial.* "I don't know. I just think one shouldn't have to wear goggles and a hard hat when listening to music," she said. It was not a bad song and she didn't feel that strongly about it, only sorry for her own paltry tunes, but the man's face fell, and he turned away, with his child staring gloomily at her over his shoulder.

She ordered a Venti latte, and while she was waiting, she read the top fold from the top paper in the stack below the shrink-wrapped CDs by the register. When she finished, she discreetly turned the paper over and read the bottom fold. This daily, fractured way of learning the front-page news—they had no Internet connection—she had gotten used to and even sighed about amusingly. *Be resourceful!* So their old newsletter had advised. This way of bringing Dench his morning coffee (she drank her half while walking back, burning her tongue a little) and getting the dog a walk was less resourceful than simply necessary. Sometimes she missed the greasy spoons of old, which she had still been able to find on the road when the band was touring and where a single waitress ran the register, the counter, all the tables, calling you "honey"—until you asked whether they had soy milk, at which point all endearments ceased.

Now she walked back via Princeton Place, a street she didn't usually take, but one that ran parallel to her own. Taking different routes fortified the mind, the paper had said today. This street contained a sprawling white-brick house she had seen before and had been struck by—not just its elegance and size but the magical blue sea of squill that spread across its sloped and wooded lot. She had once seen two deer there, with long tails that flicked like horses' and wagged like dogs'. And once she had seen such a deer close-up, along the road's edge on Dartmouth. It had been hit so fast it had been decapitated, and its neck lay open like a severed cable bundle.

Cat nosed along the gullies and a little up the driveways, whose cracks were often filled with clover.

She stared at the wings of the white-brick house, which were either perfectly insulated or not heated at all, since there was still unmelted snow on the roofs. Suddenly an elderly man appeared by the mailbox. "Howdy," he said. It startled her, and his stab at gregariousness belied his face, which bore a blasted-apart expression, like that of a balding, white-haired Jesus on the cross, eyes open wide and worried, his finely lined mouth the drawstring purse of the aged and fair.

"Just getting my newspaper," he said. "Nice dog."

"Hey, Catsy, get back here." She tried to pull the leash in, but its automated spring was broken and the leash kept unspooling.

The man's face brightened. He had started to take his paper out of its plastic sleeve but stopped. "What's the dog's name? Cathy?" He did not scrunch up his face disapprovingly when he failed to hear what you said, the way deaf people often did. But he did have the recognizable waxen pee smell of an old man. It was from sweat that no longer could be liquid but accumulated like scaly air on the skin.

"Uh, Cat. It's part family name, part, um, joke." She wasn't going to get into all the Katherines in her family or her personal refrigerator magnet altar to Cat Power or the general sick sense of humor that had led this dog, like all pets, to be a canvas upon which one wrote one's warped love and dubious wit.

"I get it." He grinned eagerly. "And what's your name?"

"KC," she said. Let that suffice.

"Casey?"

"Yes," she said. A life could rhyme with a life—it could be a jostling close call that one mistook for the thing itself.

"We live the next block over. We're renting."

"Renting! Well, that explains it."

She didn't dare ask what it explained. Still, his eyes had a wet dazzle—or an amused glint—and were not disapproving. Cat started to bark loudly at a rabbit but then also turned and started barking at the man, who took a theatrical step back, raised the paper over his head, and pretended to be afraid, as if he were performing for a small child. "Don't take my crossword puzzle!"

"His bark is worse than his bite," KC said. "Get over here, Cat."

"I don't know why people always say that. No bark is worse than a bite. A bite is always worse."

"Well, they shouldn't make rabbits so cute or we wouldn't care if dogs ate them. Why are rabbits made so cute? What is nature's purpose in that one?"

He beamed. "So you're a philosopher!"

"No, not really," she murmured as if in fact she thought she might be.

"I think the rabbits are probably only accidentally cute to us. Mostly they're cute to each other. The purpose? The new urban pest made palatable: more rabbit stew for everybody."

"I see. So you're a sort of Mr. McGregor kind of guy. I was always scared of Mr. McGregor!" She smiled.

"Nothing to be scared of. But it does seem of late that there is some kind of apocalyptic plague of rabbits. Biblical bunnies! Would you like to come and finish your coffee inside?"

She didn't know what to make of this invitation. Was it creepy or friendly? Who could tell anymore? Very few people had been friendly to them since they'd moved here two months ago. The man's tea-stained teeth made a sepia smile—a dental X-ray from the nineteenth century.

"Oh, thanks, I really should be going." This time the leash caught and Cat came trotting toward her, bored and ready to move on.

"Well, good to meet you," the old man said and turned and walked back toward his house, with its portico and porch and two stone chimneys, its wings that stretched east and west and one out back smaller and south-facing, with a long double sleeping porch, she could barely see. Over here on Princeton Place things seemed bigger than they were on Wellesley Way. She hated money! though she knew it was like blood and you needed it. Still, it was also like blood in that she often couldn't stand the sight of it. This whole privileged neighborhood could use a neat little guillotine or some feed-capped crowds with pitchforks.

"Good to meet you," she said, though he hadn't given her his name.

"Here's your coffee," she said to Dench, who was still in bed.

"Yum. Tepid backwash."

"Hey, don't complain. You can go next time and bring me back half."

"I'm not complaining," he said in a sleepy stretch. "But it's like it took you longer this time."

She took a brush sharply to her scalp and began brushing. If she waited longer with her hair she might get twelve hundred. She threw it back and arched from her waist. Only in the mirror could she see her *Decatur* tattoo, put there one night in

Linotype Gotharda in the crook of her neck, when they were playing in Decatur and she wanted to be reminded never to play there again. "That's a strange way to be reminded," Dench had said, and KC had said, "What better?"

"Was there a big line at the coffee shop?" Dench asked, smacking his lips.

"No. I stopped and talked to some guy. Cat is going up every driveway that ever had a squirrel or rabbit dash over it."

"Some guy?"

"Geezer."

"Hey, this backwash is good. There's something new in it. Were you wearing cherry ChapStick or something?"

"Have you noticed that there are a lot of people with money around here?"

"We should meet them. We need producers."

"You go meet them." She would look up *guillotine* on the Internet on her next trip to the library.

"You're cuter. Of course, time is of the essence in these matters."

She loved Dench. She was helpless before the whole emotional project of him. But it didn't preclude hating him and everything around him, which included herself, the sound of her own voice—and the sound of his, which was worse. The portraits of hell never ceased and sometimes were done up in raucous, gilded frames to console. Romantic hope: From where did women get it? Certainly not from men, who were walking caveat emptors. No, women got it from other women, because in the end women would rather be rid of one another than have to endure themselves on a daily basis. So they urged each other into relationships. "He loves you! You can see it in his eyes!" they lied.

———

"Casey!" the old man shouted the next morning. He was out in his front yard pounding together something that looked like a bird feeder on a post.

"Hi!" she said.

"You know my name?"

"Pardon me?"

"Old family joke." He still seemed to be shouting. "Actually my name is Milton Theale."

"Milton." She repeated the name, a habit people with good memories supposedly relied on. "They don't name kids Milton anymore."

"Too bad and thank God! My father's name was Hi, short for Hiram, and now that I'm old I find my head filled up with *his* jokes and stories rather than very many of my own, which apparently I've forgotten."

"Oh," she said. "Well, as long as you don't actually come to believe you are your dad, I suppose all is well."

"Well, that may be next."

"Probably that's always next. For all of us."

He squinted to study her, seemed to be admiring something about her again, but she was not sure what. No doubt something that was a complete mirage.

"Nice to see you again," he said. "And you, too," he said to the dog. "Though you are a strange-looking thing. It's like he's been assembled by Nazi veterinarians—a shepherd's head, a dachshund's body, a—"

"Yeah, I know. Sometimes he reminds me of the dog in *Invasion of the Body Snatchers*."

"Hmmm?"

"The remake."

"The remake of what?"

"Frankenstein!" she yelled. His deafness would give her a heart attack. Perhaps this was nature's plan for old people to kill each other in an efficient if irritating fashion.

She could feel the heat leaving the coffee and entering her hand. "He's like a dog made in Frankenstein's lab!" Sometimes she hated the dog. His obliviousness to the needs of others, his determined, verbally challenged conversation about his own desires—in a human this would indicate a severe personality disorder.

"Oh, he's not that bad," said Milt. "And wouldn't we like his energy. In tablet form."

"That would be fantastic."

"But you're young; you wouldn't need something like that."

"I need something." Was she whining? She had never made such an announcement to a stranger before.

"In lieu of that, come on in and have a blueberry muffin with me." Again, the line between neighborliness and flirtation was not clear to her here. She knew in this community you had to do an extroverted kind of meet and greet, but she had heard of soccer parents wandering off from their children's games and having sex in far parking lots. So the guidelines were murky and breachable. "And while you're at it you can help me with the crossword puzzle."

"Oh, I can't. I have to get home. Lot of things to tend to."

"Well, it's not ten to. It's ten past."

"To *tend* to," KC repeated. Perhaps his deafness had exhausted all the other neighbors and this accounted for his friendliness to her. On the other hand, no one seemed to walk around here. Either they jogged, their ears stuffed with music, or they drove their cars at murderous speeds. One old man could not have single-handedly caused that. Or could he have?

"Hmmm?"

"Gotta get home."

"Oh, OK," he said and waved her on.

"Maybe tomorrow," she said out of kindness.

He nodded and went back to work.

She stopped and turned. "Are you making a bird feeder?"

"No, it's a book nook! I'll put books inside and people can help themselves. Like a little library. Now that the bookstore is closed. I'm just adjusting the clasp."

"How lovely." It was a varnished pine angled to look like the ski chalet of a doll.

"Giving the old guy a thrill? Good idea."

"What's wrong with you?"

"I'm just saying," said Dench in a hushed tone. "He's probably loaded. And gonna keel soon. And . . ."

"Stop." This was the grifter in Dench, something violent in the name of freedom, like his father, who had fled through the men's room window. "Don't say another word."

"Hey—I'm not talking about murdering him! I'm just saying you could spend a little time, make him happy, and then the end result might be, well . . . we'd all be a little happier. Where's the harm?"

"You've really gone over to the dark side." He could be shameless. Perhaps shamelessness kept bitterness at bay. Not a

chance Dench could ever be bitter. Never even post-bitter. Bitterness came when one had done the long good thing and then
gone unrewarded. Dench would never operate that way. She,
on the other hand, had been born with a sort of pre-bitterness,
casting about for the good and unacknowledged deed that
would explain her feelings—and not coming up with it. So
instead a sourness could beset her, which she had to appease
and shrink with ice cream and biographies of Billie Holiday.

"Hey, wasn't it you who wrote, 'Get your hands on some
real meat'?" Now he began to sing. "'An old shoe can be made
chewy like game / but it takes a raftload of herbs and it's just
not the same.' You wrote that."

"That was a love song to a chef. Before I knew you."

"It's good. It's got existentialism *and* advice." His eyes
avoided hers.

"You're pimping me. Is this what you call your 'talent for
life'?" He had once boasted he possessed such a thing.

"It's a working view."

"You'd better be careful, Dench. I take your suggestions
seriously."

He paused and looked at her, sternness in one eye and gen-
tleness in the other. "Well, my first piece of advice is don't take
my advice. And there's more where that came from."

"There's a smell in the house. Yeasty and sulfuric. Can you
smell it?" She looked at Dench with concern, but he seemed
to have none.

"The zeitgeist!"

"Something rotting in the walls."

"Meat or shoe?"

"Something that died in the winter and now that it's spring

is decaying in the floorboards or some crawl space or one of the walls of this room."

"Maybe my allergies are acting up. But I think I have smelled it along this side of the house, on warmer days, out there trying to get better cell phone reception. A cabbagey cheese smell: goaty with a kind of ammonia rot."

She reached for a sip of Dench's coffee.

"He probably has adult children who will inherit everything."

"Probably," said Dench, turning away and then looking back at her to study her face.

"What?" she asked.

"Nothing," he said.

Dench's sexiness, his frugal, spirited cooking (though he was no Jim Barber), his brooding gaze, his self-deprecating humor, all had lured her in. But it was like walking into a beautiful house to find the rooms all empty. In those beginning years she often saw him locking eyes with others, as if in some pact. He still had no money. She paid. At times he glanced at her with bewildering scorn. There was, in short, little romantic love. No conversation of tender feelings. Just attachment. Just the power of his voice when it spoke of things that had nothing to do with them, when it churned round and round on its loop about his childhood dogs, misdeeds, and rages at his lot. He was attractive. He was amusing. But he was not emotionally well. Intimacy was not his strong suit. "Clubs and spades," he joked. "Not diamonds, not hearts. Red cards—I just see red. They throw me out of the game every time."

"Shut up and drink your beer."

Where were the drugs?

She could see he felt sometimes that he could prey upon her insecurities and still be taken in and cared for by her. Was not the news always full of one beautiful young movie star after another thrown over for some younger and more beautiful movie star? What hope was there for ordinary women? He required a patroness but had mistakenly auditioned for her. If she possessed fewer psychic wounds than he had hoped for in a woman her age, or at least different ones, he would attempt to create some. But she was less woundable than he might think. She had not had a father who had to see a man about a horse. She in fact had a father who'd been killed by a car named after a horse. Along with her mother. A Mustang! How weird was that? Well, she had been a baby and hadn't had to deal with it.

Her grandmother had almost never mentioned her mother. Or her father. They had been scurrying across a street to get home, holding hands, which had fatally slowed them down.

Where were the drugs?

Patience was a chemical. Derived from a mineral. Derived from a star. She felt she had a bit of it. But it was not always fruitful, or fruitful with the right fruit. Once she had found a letter in Dench's coat—it was a draft in his writing with his recognizable cross-outs and it began, *It has always been hard for me to say, but your love has meant the world to me.* She did not read to the end but stuffed it back inside the coat pocket, not wanting to ruin things for him or the moving surprise of it for herself. She would let him finish his composing and choose the delivery time. But the letter never arrived or showed up for her in any manner whatsoever. She waited for months. When she finally asked about it, in a general way, he looked at her with derision and said, "I have no idea what you're talking about."

Inside the old man's house wide doorways led to shaded rooms, corridors to stairways to more corridors. Whole areas of the house were closed off with ivory quilts hung with clipped rings from fishing spears—to save on heating, she quickly surmised. There were stacks of reading material—a not uncozy clutter of magazines, some opened and abandoned, and piles of books, both new and used. On top of one was a dried-out spider plant that looked—as they used to say with blithe heartlessness of all their dying spider plants—like Bob Marley on chemo. She recognized the panic at even a moment's boredom that all these piles contained, as well as the unreasonable hopefulness regarding time. In a far room she spied a piano, an old Mason & Hamlin grand, its ebony surface matte with dust, and wondered if it was tuned. Its lid was down and stacks of newspaper sat on top.

"Don't mind the clutter, just follow me through it—the muffins are in the kitchen," he said. She followed his swaying gait into the back of the house. Beneath the wisps of white hair his skull was shiny and his scalp had the large brown spots of a giraffe—if only they weren't signs of looming death they would look appealing and whimsical and young people would probably want them—give me a liver spot!—as tattoos. Smaller versions freckled his hands. "I keep hoping this clutter is charming and not a sign of senility. I find myself not able to tell."

"It's like a bookstore or a thrift shop. That kind of clutter is always charming."

"Really?"

"Perhaps you could go all the way and put little price tags on everything." A shaming heat flushed her face.

"Ha! Well, that was partly the idea with the book nook out front. That I could put some of this to use. But feel free to add your own. All contributions welcome." The muffins were store-bought ones he had reheated in a microwave. He had not really made them at all. "I shop sparingly. You never know how long you've got. I don't even buy green bananas. That's investing with reckless hope in the future."

"Very funny."

"Is it?" He was searching her face.

"Well, I mean . . . yes, it is."

"Would you like some coffee, or do you want to just stick with your own?" He signaled with his head toward the paper cup she still held, with its white plastic top and its warted brown vest made of recycled paper bags. She looked on the counter and saw that it was instant coffee he meant, a jar of Nescafé near the stove. He turned the burner on, and gas flamed into the blue spikes of a bachelor's button beneath the kettle.

"Oh, this is fine," KC said. What did she care if Dench got no coffee today? He would prefer this mission of neighborly friendliness.

She sat down at Milt's table and he placed the muffin on a plate in front of her. Then he sat down himself. "So tell me about yourself," he said, then grinned wanly. "What brings you to this neighborhood?"

"Do I stand out that much?"

"I'm afraid you do. And not just because of those tattoos."

She only had three. She would explain them all to him later, which was what they were for: each was a story. There was

"Decatur" along her neck, the vow never to return there. There was also a "Moline" one along her collarbone—a vow never to return there. The "Swanee" along her left biceps was because she liked the chord ascension in that song, a cry of homesickness the band had deconstructed and electrified into a sneer. It was sometimes their encore. When there was one. It was also a vow never to return there. She mostly forgot about all these places until she looked into a mirror after a bath.

"My music career didn't work out and I'm subletting here. I came back to this town because this is where I used to visit my grandmother in a nursing home when I was young. I liked the lake. And she was in a place that looked out onto it and when I went to see her I would go into a large room with large windows and she would race over in her wheelchair. She was the fastest one there with the chairs."

He smiled at her. "I know exactly the place you mean. It's got a hospice wing in it called Memory Station. Though no one in it can recall a thing."

KC stuffed the muffin in her mouth and flattened its moist crenellated paper into a semicircle.

"What kind of music do you play? Is it loud and angry?" he asked with a grin.

"Sometimes," she said, chewing. "But sometimes it was gentle and musing." Past tense. Her band was dead and it hadn't even taken a plane crash to do it because they hadn't been able to afford to fly except once. "I'll come by and play something for you sometime."

His face brightened. "I'll get the piano tuned," he said.

———

There was that smell again, thawing with the final remnants of winter, in their walls. This was the sort of neighborhood where one would scarcely smell a rancid onion in a trash can. But now this strange meaty rot, with its overtones of Roquefort.

"What do you really think that is?'" KC asked Dench through the bathroom door. The change of seasons had brought new viruses and he was waterboarding himself with a neti pot.

"What?"

"The smell," she said.

"I can't smell anything right now—my nose is too congested."

She peeked into the bathroom to see him leaning sideways with the plastic pot, water running down his lips and chin. "Are you disclosing national security secrets?"

"No fucking way!" he exclaimed. "The netis will never learn a thing from me."

"You can take a book or leave it. There is a simple latch, no lock." The honey-hued planes of the hutch, angled like a bird feeder, might indeed attract birds if it didn't soon fill up with books and the clasp was not shut.

"Let's see what you have in there already." She moved in close to him. His waxy smell did not bother her.

"Oh, not much really." An old copy of *The Swiss Family Robinson* and one of *Infinite Jest*. "I'm aiming for the kids," he said. He had put up a sign that said, TAKE IT OR LEAVE IT BOOK-NOOK: HAVE A LOOK. As with a community bicycle, you could take one and never have to bring it back. Dench himself had a community bike from several communities ago. "Now that the bookstore has gone under, and with the hospital so close, I thought people might need something to read."

In addition to the elegance of the wood, there was something antique and sweet in all this—far be it from her to bring up the topic of electronic downloads.

"Probably there is a German word for the feeling of fondness one gets towards one's house the more one fixes it up for resale."

"Hausengeltenschmerz," said KC.

But he did not laugh. He was thinking. "My wife would have known," he said.

His wife had been a doctor. He told KC this now as she ate another muffin in his kitchen. It had been a second marriage for his wife and so there was a bit of sunset in it for them both: he had been stuck in his bachelor ways and hadn't married until he was sixty.

("Bachelor ways!" Dench would seize on later. "You see what he's doing?")

"She was a worldly and brilliant woman, an oncologist devoted to family medicine and public health policy," said Milt.

There was a long silence as KC watched him reminisce, his face wincing slightly as his mind sifted through the files.

"I never got on with her daughters much. But she herself, well, she was the love of my life, even if she came late to it and left early. She died two years ago. When it came it was a blessing really. I suppose. I suppose that's what one should say."

"I'm sorry."

"Thank you. But she was brilliant company. My brain's a chunk of mud next to hers." He stared at KC. "It's lonely in this neck of the woods."

She picked off a moist crumb from the front of her jacket. "But you must have friends here?" she said, and then she put the crumb quickly in her mouth.

"Well, by 'neck of the woods,' I mean old age."

"I sort of knew that, I guess," she said. "Do you have friends your age?"

"There are no humans alive my age!" He grinned his sepia teeth at her.

"Come on." Her muffin was gone and she was eyeing the others.

"I may be older than I seem. I don't know what I seem."

She would fall for the bait. "Thirty-five," she said, smiling only a little.

"Ha! Well, that's the sad thing about growing too old: there's no one at your funeral."

She always said thirty-five, even to children. No one minded being thirty-five, especially kindergartners and the elderly. No one at all. She herself would give a toe or two to be thirty-five again. She would give three toes.

He looked at her warmly. "I once studied acting and I've kept my voice from getting that quavery thing of old people."

"You'll have to teach me."

"You have a lovely voice. I take note of voices. Despite my deafness and my tinnitus. Which is a nice substitute for crickets, by the way, if you miss them in the winter. Sometimes I've got so much whistling going on in my ears I could probably fly around the room if it weren't for these heavy orthopedic shoes. Were you the singer in your band?"

"How did you know?" She slapped her hand down on the table as if this were a miracle.

"There's a way you have of wafting in and hitting the sounds of the words rather than the words themselves. I mean to clean off this piano and get you to sing."

"Oh, I don't think so. I'm very much out of tune. Probably more than the piano. As I said, my career's a little stalled right now: we need some luck, you know? Without luck the whole thing's just a thought experiment!"

"We?"

"My musical partner." She swallowed and chewed though her mouth was empty. He was a partner. He was musical. What was wrong with her? Would she keep Dench a secret from Milt?

Dench would want it. "What can I get for you?" she had asked Dench this morning, and he had stared at her balefully from the bed.

"You have a lot of different nightgowns," Dench had replied.

"They're all the dresses I once wore onstage." And as she had gotten dressed for her walk, he'd said, "Don't forget the coffee this time. Last time you forgot the coffee."

"It's good to have a business partner," Milt said now. "But it isn't everything."

"He's sort of a genius," she lied. Did she feel the need to put Dench in competition with Milt's dead wife?

"So you've met some geniuses." He smiled. "You're having fun then. A life with geniuses in it: very good."

She lived with so much mockery this did not bother her at all. She looked deeply into his eyes and found the muck-speckled blue there, the lenses cut out from cataracts. She would see the cut edges in the light.

———

"Do you think our landlord, Ian, would miss a few of his books?"

"No one misses a few of their books. It's just the naked truth. Look at the sign down the road," Dench said.

The out-of-business Borders with its missing *d*: perhaps Dench had stolen it for himself, stashing it under the bed; she didn't dare look.

"Old Milt has a little book nook—I thought I'd contribute."

"I see."

"I'd only take a few. I can't donate my own since they all have the most embarrassing underlinings. In ink." Plus exclamation points that ran down the page like a fence by Christo. Perhaps it was genetic. She had once found in her grandmother's shelves her mother's own frighteningly marked-up copy of *The House of Mirth*. The word *whoa* appeared on every other page.

"Come here. Lie on top of me." Dench's face was a cross between longing and ordering lunch.

"I'll squash you. I've gained five pounds eating muffins with Milt." He grabbed her hand, but she gently pulled it away. "Give me some time. I'm going to cut out the sweets and have a few toes removed."

She had put on a necklace, of freshwater pearls so small they were like grains of arborio rice decorating the letters of *Decatur*. She combed a little rat's nest into the crown of her hair to perk it up. She dabbed on some scent: fig was the new vanilla! As she went out the door, Dench said, "Win them with your beauty, but catch them off guard with your soul." Then there was the pregnant pause, the instruments all cutting out at once—until he added, in a chilly tone, "Don't even bother with my coffee. I mean really: don't bother." After that she heard only her own footsteps.

"I brought you a couple books," she said to Milton. "For your nook."

"Well, thank you. Haven't had any takers yet but there's still room." He looked at the titles she had brought: *Collapse: How Societies Choose to Fail or Succeed* and *Lady Macbeth in the Gilded Age*. "Excellent."

They once again went inside and ate muffins. Forget coffee: this time she had not even brought the dog.

She began to do this regularly, supplying Milt with more of her landlord's books. He had taken to looking so happy to see her, his eyes brightening (blue, she had read once, was the true color of the sun) so much she could see what he must have looked like when he was young. He was probably the bachelor that all the old ladies were after. And when he had married there were probably some broken hearts. He had the look of a gentleman, but one who was used to the attention of women, even as the uriny smell of an old man had crept over him. "Here we are: two lonely fools," he said to KC once. It had the sound of a line he'd said before. Nonetheless, she found herself opening up to him, telling him of her life, and he was sympathetic, nodding, his peeled-back eyes taking on a special shine, and only once or twice did he have to lean forward disconcertingly to murmur, "Say that again?" She didn't mention Dench anymore. And the part of her that might consider this and know why was overshadowed by the unknowing part, which she knew in advance was the only source of any self-forgiveness. Ignorance ironically arranged for future self-knowledge. Life was never perfect.

When she twice stayed into the afternoon to fix Milt something to eat and once stopped by later to cook a simple dinner, Dench confronted her. "Once more I must ask: What are you doing?"

"He's a frail old man on the outs with his stepdaughters. He could use someone to help him with meals."

"You're fattening him for the kill?" They were looking into the abyss of the other, or so they both probably thought.

"What the hell are you talking about? He's alone!"

"A lone what?"

"A lone ranger for God's sake, what is wrong with you?"

"I don't understand what you're pretending."

"I'm not pretending. What I don't get is you: I thought I was doing what you wanted!"

He tilted his head quizzically the way he sometimes did when he was pretending to be a different person. Who are you doing that head-tilt thing for, she did not say.

"I don't know what I want," he said. "And I don't know what you're doing."

"You know exactly what I'm doing."

"Is that what you think? Hmmmm. Are we always such a mystery to ourselves and to others?"

"Is a disappointment the same as a mystery?"

"A disappointment is rarely a mystery."

"I'm starting to lose confidence in you, Dench." Losing confidence was more violent than losing love. Losing love was a slow dying, but losing confidence was a quick coup, a floor that opened right up and swallowed.

Now he lifted his face beatifically, as if to catch some light no one else could see. His eyes closed, and he began rubbing his hands through his hair. It was her least favorite thing that he did in the head-tilting department.

"Sorry to interrupt your self-massage," she said and turned to go and then turned back to say, "And don't give me that line about someone has to do it."

"Someone doesn't have to. But someone should." The muttered snark in their house was a kind of creature—perhaps the one in their walls.

"Yes, well, you're an expert on *should*."

It broke her heart that they had come to this: if one knew the future, all the unexpected glimpses of the beloved, one might have trouble finding the courage to go on. This was probably the reason nine-tenths of the human brain had been rendered useless: to make you stupidly intrepid. One was working with only the animal brain, the Pringle brain. The wizard-god brain, the one that could see the future and move objects without touching them, was asleep. Fucking bastard.

The books she brought this time were *Instinct for Death* and *The Fin de Millennial Lear.* She and Milt stood before the nook and placed the volumes inside.

"Now you must come in and play the piano for me. At long last I've had it tuned." Milt smiled. "You are even allowed to sing, if you so desire."

She was starting again to see how large the house was, since if they entered through a different door she had no idea where she was. There were two side doors and a back one in addition to the front two. Two front doors! Life was hard enough—having to make that kind of decision every day could wear a person out.

She sat down at the piano, with its bell-like sound and real ivory keys, chipped and grainy. As a joke she played "The Spinning Song," but he didn't laugh, only smiled, as if perhaps it were Scarlatti. Then she played and sang her love song to the chef, and then she did "Body and Soul" and then her own deconstructed version of "Down by the River," right there inside the house with no requests to leave and go down by an actual river. And then she thought that was probably enough and pulled her arms back, closed her mouth, and in imitation of Dench closed her eyes, lifted her face to the ceiling, and smoothed back her hair, prepping it for the wig maker. Then she shook her arms in the air and popped her eyes open.

Milt looked happier than she had ever seen him look. "Marvelous!" he said.

No one ever said *marvelous* anymore.

"Oh, you're nice," she said.

"I have an idea! Can you drive me downtown? I have an appointment in a half hour and I'd like you to come with me. Besides, I'm not allowed to drive."

"All right," she said. Of course she had guessed that soon she might be taking him to doctors' appointments.

Instead, she drove him in his old, scarcely used Audi, which she found stored in the garage with a dust cloth over it, to his lawyer's. "Meet my lovely new friend, Casey," he said, introducing her as they were ushered into the lawyer's gleaming office and the lawyer stared at her skeptically but shook her hand.

"Rick, I would like to change my will," Milt said.

"Yes, I know. You wanted to—"

"No, now I want to change it even more than I said before. I know we were going to leave the house to the Children's Hospital, which was Rachel's wish, but they're doing fine without us, their machinery's over there tearing things up every day on that new wing. So instead I'd like to leave everything, absolutely everything, to Casey here. And to make her executor as well."

Silence fell over the room as Milt's beaming face went back and forth between pale-feeling KC and pale-looking Rick.

"Milt, I don't think that's a good idea," KC said, clutching his arm. It was the first time she had actually touched him and it seemed to energize him further.

"Nonsense!" he said. "I want to free you from any burdens— it will keep you the angel you are."

"It hardly seems that *I'm* the angel."

"You are, you are. And I want you and your music to fly untethered."

Rick gave her a wary look as he made his way slowly behind a mahogany desk the size of a truck flatbed. He sat down in a leather chair that had ball bearings and a reclining mechanism that he illustrated by immediately beginning to bounce against it and spin slightly, his arms now folded behind his neck. Then he threw himself forward onto a leather-edged blotter and grabbed the folder he had in front of him. "Well, I can get Maryanne to change everything right now." Then Rick studied KC again, and in a voice borrowed from either his youth or his son, said to her, "Nice tats."

She did not speak of it to Dench. She did not know how. She thought of being wry—hey, Villa is back! and this time it's an actual villa—but there was no good way. She had been passive before Milt's gift—gifts required some passivity—and she would remain passive before Dench. Besides, the whole situation could change on a dime, and she half hoped it would. Like almost everything, it existed in the hypothetical—God only knew how many times Milt had changed his will—so she would try not to think of it at all. Except in this way: Milt had

no one. And now he had no one but her. Which was like having no one.

Dench appeared in the bathroom doorway as she was cutting
bangs into her hair with nail scissors. "I thought you were growing your hair," he said. "I thought you were going to sell it."

"It's just bangs," she said, threw down the scissors, and
brushed past him.

She began to take Milt to his doctors' appointments, though
she sat in the waiting room. "I've got reservations both at the
hospice wing where your grandmother was and also right
there," he said as they passed the Heavenly Sunset Cemetery.

"Do you have a good tree?"

"What?"

"Do you have a good space beneath a strong tree?" she said
loudly.

"I do!" he exclaimed. "I'm next to my wife." He paused,
brooding. "Of course she has on her gravestone ALONE AT LAST.
So, I'm putting on mine NOT SO FAST."

KC laughed, which she knew was what he wanted. "It's good
to have a place."

At the doctor's sometimes the nurse, and sometimes the phy-
sician's assistant, would walk him back out to her and give her
hurried and worried instructions. "Here is his new medicine,"
they would say, "but if he has a bad response we'll put him back
on the other one." Milt would shrug as if he were surrounded
by a gaggle of crazy relatives.

Once, a nurse leaned in and whispered, "There's a fear it
may have spread to the brain. If you have any trouble on the

weekend, phone the hospital or even the hospice. Watch his balance particularly."

KC took another of Ian's books to Milt's book nook, and one day, not seeing the old man outside, she worriedly tied Cat to the book nook post, went up to the main door, and knocked. She opened it and stepped in. "Hello? Good morning? Milt?"

Out stepped a middle-aged woman with an authoritative stride. Her heels hit the floorboards and stopped. She wore black slacks and a white shirt tucked into the waistband. Her hair was cut short—thick and gray. It was the sort of hair that years ago, when it was dark, wigmakers would have paid good money for. The woman stood there staring for a long time and then said, "I know what you're up to."

"What are you talking about?"

"One of his Concertos in Be Minor. How old are you?"

"I'm thirty-eight."

"I wonder if he knows that. You look younger."

"Well, I'm not."

"Hence your needs."

"I don't know what you mean."

"No? You don't?"

"No." Denial, when one was accused, was a life force, and would trump any desire to confess. Perhaps this was the animal strength of the psychopathic brain. Or the psychopathy of the animal brain. An admission of guilt would knock the strength right out of you—making it easier for them to twist your arms behind you and put the handcuffs on. It was from Dench, perhaps, that she had learned this.

"Shall we sit?" The pewter-haired woman motioned toward one of the sofas.

"I don't think that's necessary."

"You don't."

"No, besides, I was just walking my dog, and he's still tied up outside. I was just checking on Milt."

"Well, my sister has taken him to his doctor's appointment, so he won't be needing you today."

In bed KC lay next to Dench, staring at the ceiling, and smoking a cigarette, though they were not supposed to smoke inside. Cat lay on the quilt at the foot of the bed, doing his open-eyed fake-sleep. They were all carnies at the close of Labor Day. She stared at her Hammond keyboard, which right now had laundry piled and draped over it in angles. "What illness do you suppose Milt actually has?" Dench asked.

"Something quiet but wretched."

"Early onset quelque chose?"

"Not that early. I don't think I can go on visiting him anymore. I just can't do it."

Dench squeezed her thigh then caressed it. "Sure you can," he said.

She stabbed out her cigarette in a coffee cup, then, turning, rubbed her hand down along Dench's sinewy biceps and across his tightly muscled stomach, feeling hounded back into his arms, which she had never really left, and now his arms' familiarity was her only joy. You could lose someone a little but they would still roam the earth. The end of love was one big zombie movie.

"Do you realize that if you smoke enough you will end up lowering your risk of uterine cancer?" she said.

"That's a bad one," said Dench. "The silent killer. Especially in men."

"What did you do today?"

"I worked on some songs about my slavery-oppressed ancestors. I'm blaming the white man for my troubles."

She thought of his father. "Well, in your case it's definitely a white man."

"For most people it is. That's why we need more songs."

"Life! It's a hell of a thing, isn't it."

"I wouldn't have voted for it. I wouldn't give it any stars. It's like getting a book where the sexy passages are already underlined. Who wants that?"

She wasn't sure what he meant. But she kissed him on his shoulder anyway. "Wouldn't it be lovely just to fly out of here and live far away on a cloud together?"

"To be birds and see Gawwd!"

She had given up trying to determine his facetiousness level. She suspected it was all just habit and his true intent was unknown even to himself. "Yes! We could be birds in a little birdhouse that had books and we could read them!" she exclaimed.

Dench turned his head quickly on the pillow to stare at her. "Perhaps we have that already," he said. "But darlin, we ain't seeing God."

"Because God is off in some cybercafé, so tired from all those biblical escapades that now he just wants to sit back and Google himself all day." She pulled her hand away from Dench since he had not reciprocated with his own. "If he's not completely deaf to our cries, he's certainly deaf in one ear."

"For sure. Not just the hardware of the inner ear but the hairs and jelly further in: all shot."

"You're a strange boy."

"You see? We're getting past the glaze and right down to the factory paint here."

She let a few days go by and then she resumed her stopping by at Milt's on her coffee runs. Because summer had set in she was now bringing Dench iced coffee, but invariably the ice cubes would melt and she would just drink the whole thing herself. Milt still heated up his muffins but often needed her to drive him to doctors' appointments as well as to other places, and so she ran his errands with him and watched him greet all the salespeople, the druggist, the dry-cleaning girl, all of whom he seemed to know. "I'm so glad my wife's daughters are gone," he said at one point as they were driving home. "I dread the house with them there. I'd rather just return to the cave of my own aloneness!"

"I know how you feel."

"You have no idea," he said and leaned in to kiss her on the cheek before he got out of the car. "They are as cold as they come. I mean, even the ice on Mars melts in springtime!"

Once she took the old man swimming. They went to a beach farther north on the lake, at a state park on a weekday, when there was no one there. "Don't look!" he squealed as he took off his shirt and limp-jogged into the water, where he was safer than he was on land. He was not in bad shape, merely covered with liver spots, and his stomach was only slightly rounded and his breasts about the size of her own.

"How's the water?" she called to him. A line of silver at the water's edge sparkled in the sun. The sky was the deep belligerent blue of a hyacinth.

"Expect the unexpected!" he called back. She could see he'd once been a strong swimmer. His arms moved surely, bold, precise. Of course, when you expected the unexpected, it was no longer unexpected, and so you were not really following instructions. She admired his gameness. As she approached the water she saw that the silver line along the sand was the early die-off of the alewives: washed ashore gasping and still flipping on your foot as you walked. The dead lay in a shiny line upbeach, and if one of the smelt-like fish died closer to the waves it caught the light like the foil of a gum wrapper. Another putrid perplexity of the earth. She dove out anyway—to swim among the dying. She would pretend to be an aquarium act, floating among her trained, finned minions; if she imagined it any other way it was all too disgusting. She bobbed around a bit, letting the olive waves of the lake crest up and wash over her.

They picnicked back on shore. She had brought cheese sandwiches and club soda and difficult peaches: one had to bite sharply into the thick fuzzed skin of them to get to the juice. They sat huddled in their separate towels, on a blanket, everything sprinkled with sand, their feet coated in it like brown sugar.

"Too bad about the dead fish," Milt said. "They'll be gone next week but still. So may I!" He grinned.

Should she say "Don't talk like that"? Should she in her bathing suit with her tattoos all showing feign a bourgeois squeamishness regarding conversations about death? "Please don't talk like that," she said, peach juice dripping down her chin.

"OK," he said obediently. "I'm just saying: even Nature

has her wickednesses." He took out a flask she didn't know he carried and poured her a little into a paper cup. "Here, have some gin. Goes in clean and straight—like German philosophy!" He smiled and looked out at the lake. "I was once a philosopher—just not a very good one."

"Really?" The gin stung her lips.

"Terrible world. Great sky. That always seemed the gist." He paused. "I also like bourbon—the particular parts of your brain it activates. Also good for philosophy."

She thought about this. "It's true. Bourbon hits a very different place than, say, wine."

"Absolutely."

"And actually, red wine hits a different place from white." She sipped her gin. "Not that I've made an intense study of it."

"No, of course not." He smiled and rinsed gin around on his gums.

Back at his house he seemed to have caught a chill and she put a blanket around him and he grabbed her hand. "I have to go," she said.

A sadness had overtaken him. He looked at KC then looked away. "Shortly before my wife died she sat up in bed and began to shout out the names of all the sick children who had died on her watch. I'd given her a brandy and she just began reciting the names of all the children she had failed to save. 'Charlie Pepper,' she cried, 'and Lauren Cox and Barrett Bannon and Caitlin Page and Raymond Jackson and Tom DeFugio, and little Deanna Lamb.' This went on for an hour."

"I have to go—will you be OK?" He had taken his hand away and was just staring into space. "Here is my number," she said, writing on a small scrap of paper. "Phone me if you need anything."

When he did not reply she left anyway, ignoring any anguish, locking the door from the inside.

Perhaps everyone had their own way of preparing to die. Life got you ready. Life got you sad. And then blood started coming from where it didn't used to come. People revisited the deaths of others, getting ready to meet them in the beyond. KC herself imagined dying would be full of rue: like flipping through the pages of a clearance catalog, seeing the drastic markdowns on stuff you'd paid full price for and not gotten that much use from, when all was said and done. Though all was never said and done. That was the other part about death.

"I had the dog all day," complained Dench, "which was no picnic. No day at the beach."

"Well, I had Milt. He's no kiss for Christmas."

"I don't know what I'm supposed to think about all the time you spend with him."

"According to you, you never know what to think."

"It just seems to me that if things are going to take they shouldn't take so long. By the way, I've found out what that odor is."

"Really?"

The smell, even with the warm weather ostensibly drying things out, was still in the walls. There was the occasional scurrying of squirrels in the attic. It was surprising Cat didn't jump up and start barking.

"The rot of a bad conscience."

"I really doubt that."

"Well, let me show you." He opened the hatch to the crawl space that constituted the attic. He pulled down the folding

ladder and motioned for her to climb it. "Take this flashlight
and move it around and you'll see."

She expected to find a couple of flying squirrels, dead in
each other's caped arms. But when she poked her head into
the crawl space and flashed her light around, she at first saw
nothing but dust and boxes. Then her eyes fell on it: a pile of
furry flesh with the intertwined tails of rats. They were a single
creature like a wreath and flies buzzed around them and excre-
ment bound them at the center while their bodies were arrayed
like spokes. Only one of them still had a head that moved and
it opened its mouth noiselessly.

"It's a rat king," said Dench. "They were born like that, with
their tails attached, and could never get away."

She scrambled down the ladder and shoved it back up. "That
is the most revolting thing I've ever seen."

"They're supposed to be bad luck."

"Put the hatch door back down."

"A surprise for Ian. I did phone the pest removal place, but
they charge a thousand dollars. I said, 'Where are you taking
them to, Europe?' We may just have to burn the house down.
It's completely haunted."

"Really."

"We could work up plausible deniability: *What kerosene
can?* Or, *Many people are known to go shopping while cooking
pot-au-feu.*"

She studied Dench's face as if—once again—she had no idea
who he was. Now having found the rat king, he seemed to be
the star of a horror film. He was trying to be funny all the time
and she no longer liked it, as if he were auditioning for something. Soon he might start telling Milt's jokes: *I keep thinking*

of the hereafter: I walk into a room and say, What am I here after?
She only liked Dench's Jesus jokes, since in them Jesus was kind
of an asshole, which she thought was perhaps a strong possibility in real life, and so the jokes seemed true and didn't have to
be funny and so she didn't have to laugh. "Don't ever show me
anything like that again," she said.

Cat came up and started to hump Dench's leg. "Sheesh,"
said Dench, as KC turned to leave. "He's had his balls cut off
and he still wants to date."

Summer warmed all the houses though most of them did not
have air conditioners, Ian's and Milt's included. She took Milt
one evening to a nearby café and they had to dine outside, at
a wobbly metal table near the parking lot, since the air within
was too slicing and cold. "I think I would have liked that cold
air when I was about seventeen," he said. "Now I feel heat is
good for old bones."

They ate slowly, and although the food clung to his teeth,
KC did not alert him. What would be the point? At some point,
good God, just let an old guy have food in his teeth! They ate
squash soup with caramel corn on top—molar-wrecking.

"You know," he said, chewing and looking around. "People get fired from the barbershop, a restaurant closes, this is a
slow town and still things change too fast for me. It's like those
big-screen TVs: all the bars have them now. I can't watch football on those—it feels like they're running right at me."

KC smiled but said nothing. At one point he said loudly of
his custard, "The banana flavor doesn't taste like real banana
but more like what burped banana tastes like."

She glanced over at the next table. "I kind of know what you mean," she said quietly.

"Of course old people are the stupidest. It's the thing that keeps me from wanting to live in a whole facility full of them. Just listen to them talk: listen to me talk. It's like: I've been walking around with the dumb thought for forty years and I'm still thinking it, so now I might as well say it over and over." He then again sang the praises of his wife, her generosity and social commitment, and then turned his attention to KC. "You are not unlike her, in a way," he said. Behind him the sun set in the striped hues of a rutabaga.

"I can't imagine," she said. Instead her mind was filled with wondering what the neighbors must think.

"Your faces are similar in a way. Especially when you smile!" He smiled at her when he said this and she returned it with a wan one of her own, her lips in a tight line.

When she walked him back to his house, the crickets had started in with their beautiful sawing. "Tinnitus!" Milt exclaimed.

But this time she didn't laugh, and so he did what he often did when he was irritated: he walked with his most deaf ear toward her so that he could stew in peace. She noticed him weaving and knew that his balance was off. At one point he began to tilt and she quickly caught him. "An old guy like me should wear a helmet all the time," he said. "Just get up in the morning and put it on."

He then turned and peered through the dusk at her. "Sometimes at home I think the ringing in my ears might be the phone and I pick it up, hoping it might be you."

She helped him into his house—he took the front stairs with greater difficulty than he used to. She turned on the lights. But he switched them off again and, grabbing her hand, sat in a chair. "Come here and sit on my lap," he said, tugging her firmly. She fell awkwardly across his thin thighs, and when she tried to find her footing to stand again, he braced and embraced her with his arms and began to nuzzle her neck, the *u* and *r* of *Decatur.* His eyes were closed, and he offered his face up to her, his lips pursed but moving a little to find hers.

KC at first let him kiss her, letting their lips meet slightly—she had to be obliging, she had to work against herself and find a way—and then his rough and pointed tongue flicked quickly in and out and she jolted, flung herself away, stood, switched the lights back on, and turned to face him. "That's it! You've gone off the deep end now!"

"What?" he asked. His eyes were barely open and his tongue only now stopped its animal darting. She swept her hair from her face. The room seemed to whirl. Life got you ready for dying. She had once caught a mouse in a mousetrap—she had heard the snap and when she looked it seemed merely to be a tea bag, a brown mushroomy thing with a tail, then it began flopping and flipping and she'd had to pick it up with a glove and put it in the freezer, trap and all, to die there.

It was time. "You're completely crazy!" she said loudly. "And there's nothing I can do at this point but call the hospice!" Words that had stayed in the wings now rushed into the crushed black box of her throat.

His face now bore the same blasted-apart look she'd seen when she first met him, except this time there was something mangled about the eyes, his mouth a gash, his body slumped in banishment. He began silently to cry. And then he spoke. "I looked him up on—what do you call it: Spacebook. His interests and his seekings."

"What are you talking about?"

"Good luck," he said. "Good luck to you and your young man—I wish you both the best."

"It's done."

She sank against the door. She had waited all night for the hospice people to come and carry Milt off the next morning, and then she had signed some forms and promised to visit, promised to come help him with the crossword puzzle, and taking the keys of the house, she had locked it, then walked hurriedly home.

Dench was putting his cell phone away. He looked at her worriedly and she returned his gaze with a hard glare. He then stepped forward, perhaps to comfort her, but she shoved him off. "KC," he said. And when he cocked his head as if puzzled and tried in forgiveness to step toward her again, she made a fist and struck him hard in the face.

Her life in the white-brick house was one of hostessing—and she poured into it all the milk of human kindness she possessed. There were five bedrooms and one suite turned entirely over to the families of children at the hospital whose new pediatric wing was now complete. She had painted the walls of every room either apricot or brown, and she kept the crown moldings white while she painted the ceilings a celestial blue. In summer she opened up the sleeping porches. Every morning she got up early and made breakfast, a ham-and-egg bake, which she served in a large casserole in the dining room, and although she made no other meals she made sure there were cookies in the front room and games for the siblings (who also played with the dog). She sometimes attempted music in the afternoons, sitting at the piano while people tried to smile at her. She wore high collars and long sleeves and necklaces of blue slag to hide her tattoos. She left magazines for people to read but not newspapers, which contained too much news. She maintained the book nook, stuffing it with mysteries. She watched the families as they went off in the morning, walking their way to the hospital to see their sick children. She never saw the sick children themselves—except at night, when they were ghosts in white nightgowns and would stand on the stairwell landings and recite their names and wave—as she roamed the house, thinking of them as "her children" and then not thinking of them at all, as she sleeplessly straightened up, but she would hear of their lives. "I missed the good parts," the mothers would say, "and now there are no more good parts." And she would give them more magazines for flipping through in the surgery lounge, in case they grew tired of watching a thriving aquarium of bright little fish.

Tears thickened her skin the way brine knitted and hardened the rind of a cheese. Her hair was still long but fuzzily linted with white, and she wore it up in a clip. There were times looking out the front windows, seeing the parents off on their dutiful, despairing visits, when she would think of Dench and again remember the day he had first auditioned raucously for their band, closing with some soft guitar, accompanied by his strong but inexpressive baritone, so the song had to carry the voice, like a river current moving a barge. She had forgotten now what song it was. But she remembered she had wondered whether it would be good to love him, and then she had gone broodingly to the window to look out at the street while he was singing and she had seen a very young woman waiting for him in his beat-up car. It had been winter with winter's sparse afternoon stars, and the girl was wearing a fleece chin-strap cap that made her look like Dante and also like a baby bird. KC herself had been dressed like Hooker Barbie. Why had she put this memory out of her mind? The young woman had clearly driven him there—would she be tossed away? bequeathed? forgotten? given a new purpose by God, whose persistent mad humor was aimless as a gnat? She was waiting for him to come back with something they could use.

REFERENTIAL

Mania. For the third time in three years they talked in a frantic way about what would be a suitable birthday present for her deranged son. There was so little they were actually allowed to bring: almost everything could be transformed into a weapon and so most items had to be left at the front desk, and then, if requested, brought in later by a big blond aide, who would look the objects over beforehand for their wounding possibilities. Pete had bought a basket of jams, but they were in glass jars, and so not allowed. "I forgot about that," he said. They were arranged in color from brightest marmalade to cloudberry to fig, as if they contained the urine tests of an increasingly ill person, and so she thought, *Just as well they will be confiscated.* They would find something else to bring.

By the time her son was twelve, and had begun his dazed and spellbound muttering, no longer brushing his teeth, Pete had been in their lives for four years, and now it was four years after that. The love they had for Pete was long and winding, not without hidden turns, but without any real halts. They thought of him as a kind of stepfather. Perhaps all three of them had gotten old together, although it showed mostly on her, the mother, with her black shirtdresses worn for slimming and her now graying hair undyed and often pinned up with strands hanging down like Spanish moss. Once her son had been stripped and gowned and placed in the facility, she, too, removed her necklaces, earrings, scarves—all her prosthetic devices, she said to Pete, trying to amuse—and put them in a latched accordion file under her bed. She was not allowed to wear them when visiting so she would no longer wear them at all, a kind of solidarity with her child, a kind of new widowhood on top of the widowhood she already possessed. Unlike other women her age (who tried too hard with lurid lingerie and flashing jewelry), she now felt that sort of effort was ludicrous, and she went out into the world like an Amish woman, or perhaps, even worse, as when the unforgiving light of spring hit her face, an Amish man. If she were going to be old, let her be a full-fledged citizen of the old country! "To me you always look so beautiful," Pete no longer said.

Pete had lost his job in the new economic downturn. At one point he had been poised to live with her, but her child's deepening troubles had caused him to pull back—he believed he loved her but could not find the large space he needed for himself in her life or in her house (and did not blame her son, or did he?). He eyed with somewhat visible covetousness and sour remarks the front room that her son, when home, lived in with large blankets and empty ice-cream pints, an Xbox, and DVDs.

She no longer knew where Pete went, sometimes for weeks at a time. She thought it an act of vigilance and attachment that she would not ask, would try not to care. She once grew so hungry for touch she went to the Stressed Tress salon around the corner just to have her hair washed. The few times she had flown to Buffalo to see her brother and his family, at airport security she had chosen the pat-downs and the wandings rather than the scanning machine.

"Where is Pete?" her son cried out at visits she made alone, his face scarlet with acne, swollen and wide with the effects of medications that had been changed then changed again, and she said Pete was busy today, but soon, soon, maybe next week. A maternal vertigo beset her, the room circled, and the cutting scars on her son's arms sometimes seemed to spell out Pete's name in the thin lines there, the loss of fathers etched primitively in an algebra of skin. In the carousel spin of the room, the white webbed lines resembled coarse campfire writing, as when young people used to stiffly carve the words PEACE and FUCK in park picnic tables and trees, the *C* three-quarters of a square. Mutilation was a language. And vice versa. The cutting endeared her boy to the girls, who were all cutters themselves and seldom saw a boy who was one as well, and so in the group sessions he became popular, which he seemed neither to mind nor perhaps really to notice. When no one was looking he cut the bottoms of his feet with crisp paper from crafts hour. He also pretended to read the girls' soles like palms, announcing the arrival of strangers and the progress toward romance—"toemances!" he called them—and detours, sometimes glimpsing his own fate in the words they had cut there.

Now she and Pete went to see her son without the jams but with a soft deckle-edged book about Daniel Boone, which was allowed, even if her son would believe it contained messages for him, believe that although it was a story about a long-ago person it was also the story of his own sorrow and heroism in the face of every manner of wilderness and defeat and abduction and that his own life could be draped over the book, which was noble armature for the revelation of tales of *him.* There would be clues in the words on pages with numbers that added up to his age: 97, 88, 466. There were other veiled references to his existence. There always were.

They sat at the visitors' table together and her son set the
book aside and did try to smile at both of them. There was
still sweetness in his eyes, the sweetness he was born with,
even if fury could dart in a scattershot fashion across them.
Someone had cut his tawny hair—or at least had tried. Perhaps
the staff person did not want the scissors near him for a pro-
longed period and had snipped quickly, then leaped away, then
approached again, grabbed and snipped, then jumped back. At
least that's what it looked like. It was wavy hair and had to be
cut carefully. Now it no longer cascaded down but was close to
his head, springing out at angles that seemed to matter to no
one but a mother.

"So where have you been?" her son asked Pete, giving him
a hard stare.

"Good question," said Pete, as if praising the thing would
make it go away. How could people be mentally well in such
a world?

"Do you miss us?" the boy asked.

Pete did not answer.

"Do you think of me when you look at the black capillaries
of the trees at night?"

"I suppose I do." Pete stared back at him, so as not to shift
in his seat. "I am always hoping you are OK and that they treat
you well here."

"Do you think of my mom when staring up at the clouds
and all they hold?"

Pete fell quiet again.

Her son continued, studying Pete. "Have you ever watched
how sparrows can kill the offspring of others? Baby wrens, for
instance? I've been watching out the windows. Did you know
that sparrows can swoop into the wrens' house and pluck out

the fledglings from their nests and hurl them to the ground with a force you would not think possible for a sparrow? Even a homicidal sparrow?"

"Nature can be cruel," said Pete.

"Nature can be one big horror movie! But murder is not something one would expect—from a sparrow. All things can be found in the world—but usually you have to look for them. You have to look! For instance, you have to look for us! We are sort of hidden but sort of not. We can be found. If you look in the obvious places, we can be found. We haven't disappeared, even if you want us to, we are there to—"

"That's enough," she said to her son, who turned to her with a change of expression.

"There's supposed to be cake this afternoon for someone's birthday," he said.

"That will be nice!" she said, smiling back.

"No candles, of course. Or forks. We will just have to grab the frosting and mash it into our eyes for blinding. Do you ever think about how at that moment of the candles time stands still, even as the moments carry away the smoke? It's like the fire of burning love. Do you ever wonder why so many people have things they don't deserve but how absurd all those things are to begin with? Do you really think a wish can come true if you never ever ever ever ever ever tell it to anyone?"

On the ride home she and Pete did not exchange a word, and every time she looked at his aging hands, clasped arthritically around the steering wheel, the familiar thumbs slung low in their slightly simian way, she would understand anew the desperate place they both were in, though the desperations were separate, not joined, and her eyes would then feel the stabbing pressure of tears. The last time her son had tried to do it, his method had been, in the doctor's words, morbidly ingenious. He might have succeeded but a fellow patient, a girl from group, had stopped him at the last minute. There had been blood to be mopped. Once her son had only wanted a distracting pain, but then soon he had wanted to tear a hole in himself and flee through it. Life was full of spies and preoccupying espionage. Yet the spies sometimes would flee as well and someone might have to go after them in order, paradoxically, to escape them altogether, over the rolling fields of living dream, into the early morning mountains of dawning signification.

There was a storm in front and lightning did its quick, purposeful zigzag between and in the clouds. She did not need such stark illustration that horizons could be shattered, filled with messages, broken codes, yet there it was. A spring snow began to fall with the lightning still cracking, and Pete put the windshield wipers on so that they both could peer through the cleared semicircles at the darkening road before them. She knew that the world was not created to speak just to her, and yet, as with her son, sometimes things did. The fruit trees had bloomed early, for instance, and the orchards they passed were pink, but the early warmth precluded bees, and so there would be little fruit. Most of the dangling blossoms would fall in this very storm.

When they arrived at her house and went in, Pete glanced at himself in the hallway mirror. Perhaps he needed assurance that he was alive and not the ghost he seemed.

"Would you like a drink?" she asked, hoping he would stay. "I have some good vodka. I could make you a nice White Russian!"

"Just vodka," he said reluctantly. "Straight."

She opened the freezer to find the vodka, and when she closed it again, she stood waiting there for a moment, looking at the photos she'd attached with magnets to the refrigerator. As a baby her son had looked happier than most babies. As a six-year-old he was still smiling and hamming it up, his arms and legs shooting out like starbursts, his perfectly gapped teeth flashing, his hair curling in honeyed coils. At ten his expression was already vaguely brooding and fearful, though there was light in his eyes, his lovely cousins beside him. There he was a plumpish teenager, his arm around Pete. And there in the corner he was an infant again, held by his dignified, handsome father, whom her son did not recall because he had died so long ago. All this had to be accepted. Living did not mean one joy piled upon another. It was merely the hope for less pain, hope played like a playing card upon another hope, a wish for kindnesses and mercies to emerge like kings and queens in an unexpected change of the game. One could hold the cards oneself or not: they would land the same regardless. Tenderness did not enter except in a damaged way and by luck.

"You don't want ice?"

"No," said Pete. "No thank you."

She placed two glasses of vodka on the kitchen table and there they sat.

"Perhaps this will help you sleep," she said.

"Don't know if anything can do that," he said, with a swig. Insomnia plagued him.

"I am going to bring him home tomorrow," she said. "He needs his home back, his house, his room. He is no danger to anyone."

Pete drank some more, sipping noisily. She could see he wanted no part of this, but she felt she had no choice but to proceed. "Perhaps you could help. He looks up to you."

"Help how?" asked Pete with a flash of anger. There was the clink of his glass on the table.

"We could each spend part of the night near him," she said.

The telephone rang. The Radio Shack wall phone brought almost nothing but bad news, and so its ringing sound, especially in the evening, always startled her. She repressed a shudder but still her shoulders hunched and curved. She stood.

"Hello?" she said, answering it on the third ring, her heart pounding. But the person on the other end hung up. She sat back down. "I guess it was a wrong number," she said, adding, "Perhaps you would like more vodka."

"Only a little. Then I should go."

She poured him more. She had said what she'd wanted to say and did not want to have to persuade him. She would wait for him to step forward with the right words. Unlike some of her meaner friends, who kept warning her, she believed there was a deep good side of him and she was always patient for it. What else could she be?

The phone rang again.

"Probably telemarketers," he said.

"I hate them," she said. "Hello?" she said more loudly into the receiver.

This time when the caller hung up she glanced at the number on the phone, in the lit panel where the caller ID was supposed to reveal it.

She sat back down and poured herself more vodka. "Someone is calling here from your apartment," she said.

He threw back the rest of his vodka. "I should go," he said

and got up and headed for the door. She followed him. At the door she watched him grasp the front knob and twist it firmly. He opened the door wide, blocking the mirror.

"Good night," he said. His expression had already forwarded itself to someplace far away.

She threw her arms around him to kiss him, but he turned his head abruptly so her mouth landed on his ear. She remembered he had done this evasive move eight years ago, at the beginning, when they had first met, and he was in a condition of romantic overlap.

"Thank you for coming with me," she said.

"You're welcome," he replied, then hurried down the steps to his car, which was parked at the curb out front. She did not attempt to walk him to it. She closed the door and locked it, as the telephone began to ring again. She turned off all the lights, including the porches'.

She went into the kitchen. She had not really been able to read the caller ID without reading glasses, and had invented the part about its being Pete's number, though he had made it the truth anyway, which was the black magic of lies, good guesses, and nimble bluffs. Now she braced herself. She planted her feet. "Hello?" she said, answering on the fifth ring. The plastic panel where the number should show was clouded as if by a scrim, a page of onionskin over the onion—or rather, over a picture of an onion. One depiction on top of another.

"Good evening," she said again loudly. What would burst forth? A monkey's paw. A lady. A tiger.

But there was nothing at all.

after VN

SUBJECT TO SEARCH

Tom arrived with his suitcase. Its John Kerry sticker did not even say "For President," so it seemed as if John Kerry might be the owner or designer of the bag. "I have to leave," Tom said, sitting down, scraping the chair along the pavement, setting the suitcase beneath the table.

"Before you eat?" she asked.

"No." He looked at his watch.

"Then order. Order quickly if you have to. Or you can have my salad, if you'd like." She indicated the watery romaine on her plate.

He scanned the menu, then put it down. "I can't even read right now. Is there couscous? Order me the lamb couscous. I'll be right back." He grabbed his cell phone. "I'm going to the gents'." His face had a grip of worry beneath the sun-beat skin; his body was lanky and his gait lopey but brisk as he wended his way inside. The suitcase stayed at the table, like a bomb.

She summoned the garçon with a gesture that was a hand flutter quickly pulled away lest the teacher actually call on you. She had no ear for languages—in that way she took after her mother, who once on her French honeymoon, seeing a "L'Ecole des Garçons," had remarked, "No wonder the restaurants are so good! The waiters all go to waiter school!"

"Pour mon ami, s'il vous plaît," she said, "le couscous d'agneau." Was that right? Did one pronounce both esses, or just one, or none, as in *cuckoo,* perhaps requesting a small musical bird from the park? When lamb was a food, was it a different word, the way pork and pig were? Perhaps she had ordered a living, breathing creature mewling in broth and fleece. The waiter nodded and did not say, "Anything more for you, madame?" but turned quickly and left. The outdoor tables were apparently all his this afternoon. It was April and the weather had changed into something oppressively lovely, with an urban breeze of garlic, diesel, and hyacinth. Where she ordinarily lived, there was not the same oniony, oily air of possibility as you walked down the street. Winter prairies choked the air clean. And spring was a brief, delicate thing quickly overtaken by tornadoes.

"Here," Tom said, when he returned, trying to lighten the mood. "I think you may have left your notebook in the loo."

He handed her a small open notebook, clearly his own, in which he had written the lyrics to Peggy Lee's "Fever." Exclamation marks and curlicues decorated all the lines. As did a small game of tic-tac-toe. At the bottom a page read, "Fish bite the least / when winds blow from the east" and "What is destiny, if you have to ask?" Also, "I love your hair the way it is, for chrissakes." That it seemed hilarious made her think, *This has always been the man for me.*

"I have to fly back to the States," he said. He put his elbows on the table and his head in his hands. She found the few people she'd known who moonlighted in the international intrigue business to be very high-energy, but there was also a price paid; Tom now seemed tired and defeated. He glanced up and added, "You know, the intelligence world: we're not James Bond. We're puny, putrid graspers and gropers, deciding things at home from our laptops, playing on a field that is far too large for us."

"Didn't Richard Burton make a speech like that in *The Spy Who Came in from the Cold*?"

"That was the speech."

"The laptop part?"

"You gotta let a guy improvise. Did you order?"

"Oui, monsieur."

"Merci." He smiled. She knew that he liked it when she said anything in French. His specialty was languages, including Urdu and Arabic, although only an hour and a half of Urdu, he declared, and then his mind turned into a blank blue screen. "And actually only four hours of Arabic," he said. "And maybe even only five of English: five hours is a long time to keep talking." Decades ago he had driven cars for a living, from Holland to Tehran, a drug runner (though he had not said this, she had surmised). Then he was recruited by American officials to teach the Shah's guards' children.

"What did you teach them?" she had once asked.

"Critical theory," he'd said, his face lit with a desire to amuse. "Movies and Marxism. Of course not *real* Marxism, nothing so practical as that. Nothing like here's how you kill people and throw them in a ditch. No, we did very abstract Marxism. Very ivory tower."

"Ha ha," she'd said.

"I taught the kids English," he mumbled in a defensive tone, "and some of their parents as well."

"Did you feel the Shah was all that bad?" she had asked and then received a long strange lecture on Chiang Kai-shek and the doubtful, simpleminded shelvings of various historical figures. She believed that in the photographs of the embassy hostages, the handsome blindfolded one, tall and bright-haired in the embassy doorway, was Tom. She herself had been a teenager at the time and had only decades later stumbled upon the photo online; the likeness took her breath away.

But he had said no, he had gotten out a month beforehand. The closed-then-open-again secrets of his work enchanted and paralyzed her, like the frog who fatally acclimates to the heating water.

He paid for everything in cash.

"Everyone looks bad now," he'd said. "Not just the Shah."

Now he held up the carafe of Côtes du Rhône, raised his eyebrows optimistically, and cocked his head. His hair was the color that strawberry blond became in middle age: bilious and bronze, as if it had been oxidized then striped with white like a ginger cat.

"No wine," she said. "It leads to cheese."

She had hoped to lose weight in time for this trip, but alas.

"You must not say anything if I tell you this." He paused, studied her, considering.

"Of course not." Did she look untrustworthy? Why did she not seem like a person of integrity, which she felt she was. It was gracefulness she was perhaps missing; people confused the two.

Tom poured some wine and drank. "In London they are reporting torture incidents involving American troops in a Baghdad prison. Someone took pictures. It is a disaster, and I have to get back." He took another swallow.

"Are the troops OK? What do you mean?"

"The troops are kids. They don't know what they're doing.

They're sheep." The waiter brought the couscous and Tom made a stab at his lamb. "It's all about to blow. The British papers are getting ready to go to press with it. It's going to be a scandal big as My Lai."

"My Lai? Well, let's not get carried away," she said, though who was she to utter such an airy thing?

His hand was trembling and he slurped his wine. "I'm serious. Believe me: the name of this prison will be a household word." And then he said the name, but it sounded like nonsense to her, and perhaps it was, though her terrible ear for languages made everything that was not English sound very, well, *mimsy,* as if plucked from "Jabberwocky": "the mome raths outgrabe."

He stabbed the air with his fork. "They are the same unit I was in when I was in the army thirty years ago. And taking their orders from military intelligence: the most notorious of oxymorons. I rue my time in Tehran and Cairo; I rue my ability to be consulted."

"You needed the money—"

"I'm sorry, but there are no more lecture slots available at this time!" he said, spreading his mouth into a smile that was like a star shining its far illusive light from long ago. "All slots have been filled by contestants who auditioned earlier!" She would never see him smile like that again. In truth probably she wasn't seeing it now. He looked through her a bit and lowered his voice. "I said to them, whatever you do, don't flush Korans down the toilet. Whatever you do don't have them be naked in front of a woman. Whatever you do don't involve them in any sexual horseplay whatsoever. Do not pantomime fellatio—which is probably good advice for everyone. I warned, don't take a Sharpie and write *Children of Akbar* on their foreheads or put women's underwear on their heads. Whatever you do don't try to reconstruct your memories of seeing Pilobolus at the civic center when you were eight. It will demoralize and degrade them."

She thought she could see what he was telling her. *Don't* code for *do.* It was what doctors sometimes did for the terminally ill who wanted to die: *whatever you do, don't take this entire prescription all at once with water.*

"Where did they get their ideas from then? The Internet?" Did he himself believe these prohibitions were not articulated this way as cover? When you fled one room of moral ambiguity, it was good to have a nice, overstuffed chair awaiting you in the next. But you then perhaps became your spook self, your ghost self, restless in a house you never knew was quite this haunted—and haunted by you.

"The Internet!" Tom said, scoffing. "The Internet just reflects what's already in the human mind. Perhaps a little less so. Cruelty comes naturally. It comes naturally to everyone. But if one is confused, and it's hot, one's bearings get even further lost. The desire to break something down so you can dominate it. Where did this idea come from? Whatever happened to simple cleverness? Instead we've got nude interrogations and sandbags soaked in pepper sauce?"

"But *you*—are MI."

"IM?"

She shifted in her seat. She couldn't recall if she had ordered any bread with her salad. "The whole planet is based on being at the right place at the right time," she said, lost herself.

"No! No!" he cried, seeing her eyes narrow into a squint. "They were supposed to de-conflict, not *gitmoize.*"

"You are simply a consultant. You weren't responsible," she said, unsure. Tom, she knew, had had a close childhood friend on Mohamed Atta's plane. Sitting right up in first class with the terrorists. "Oh, my God, what a horrible shock," she had said when he had told her the tale in a coffee shop back home.

"Yeah," he'd said, hopelessly, "you don't expect things like that to happen except in coach."

Now, again, she didn't know how to console him. "You're speaking as if you were Death itself."

"Perhaps I am, little girl. Let's go for a walk and see if you return." He began to rub his temples. "I'm sorry. I'm not sure what's wrong with me, but! I have a good idea for a cure," he added, smiling slightly, as if he were afraid he had made her nervous. He turned his hand into a pistol shape and placed it at his own temple, his thumb miming a trigger.

"That might only wound," she said. "It might merely blind you, and then you'd never be able to find a gun again."

"How about this?" he said and pointed his finger into his mouth. She could see the creamy yellow of his teeth, his molars with their mercury eyes.

"It's really an extreme way to get rid of headaches, and it still might not work."

"I've got it," he said and with both hands placed each trigger finger on either side of his head. "That do it?"

Laughter in the midafternoon night. The daylilies in the Plexiglas table vase had already called it a day.

"Veterinarians really have it down," she said. "It's so much more humane than human medicine—especially the endgame. They've got the right injections. No bad morphine dreams."

"That's why I'm getting my little puppy suit ready," he said.

"Ho ho."

"If you're suicidal," he said slowly, "and you *don't actually kill yourself,* you become known as 'wry.'"

He had headaches that could be debilitating, but he had always hid in his apartment when they came on so she had never seen how crippling they were. Two years later, when he had a chip implanted in his head—a headache cure, experimental, cutting-edge, but who could not think of *The Manchurian Candidate*?—she would go visit him, bring him lunch, listen to him joke about his shaved-off hair and the battery pack implanted in his chest. Someone, it seemed, was experimenting with him, but he did not say who, precisely. He was susceptible to charming leaders and group activities despite his remarks about sheep. He was also simultaneously stoical about all. Still later, when the chip was removed, sloppily, and the trembling that had begun in that café overtook the entirety of him, leaving him frail, unsteady, leaning on a cane, filling out retirement forms—"apparently I was in the control group and the control group does not experience the experiment"—she would drive up to see him in one of the cottages in the veterans' lakeside compound in the northern part of the state. But the woman at the reception desk always said, "He's just not seeing people today." Uniformed guards would check her car at the security gate, and once when she got home she found one of the guards' cell phones in her trunk. Mostly, if allowed, she would walk the grounds and seek out his cottage—he had his own, like a high-ranking officer, so his GS number was probably substantial. Still there was no response, even though he had replied by e-mail that yes it would be good to see her. He never answered the door the four times she had gone to see him and the nine times each that she had knocked.

"By the way," he added now, "make sure I don't have one of those ostensibly green funerals where they put the unpreserved body on view on a giant heap of ice in someone's blazingly sunny backyard. I want a church. Also? I have my music picked out."

"OK."

"Just plug my iPod into some speakers in the front of the chapel."

"Positioned to Genius?" A compliment, forehanded, she thought. They were so rare in life and even less often believed.

He acknowledged it with a nod, respecting her effort. "Oh," he said, "Shuffle will do."

Her own iPod would be an embarrassment: *Forbidden Broadway*, Sting, *French for Dummies*.

She looked around at the café's brass-rimmed tables and the waxy caned chairs. Then she looked back at Tom. He was in a state of pain and worry she had never seen him in before. Back in their once-shared hometown, through the years, first when he was married, then when she was married, they had looked for each other across rooms, hovered near each other at parties, for years they had done it, taut and electrified, each stealthily seeking the other out and then standing close, wineglasses in hand, spellbound by their own eagerly mustered small talk. She would study the superficially sleepy look his face would assume, atop his still-strapping figure, the lowered lids and wavy mouth, and emanating from behind it all his laserlike concentration on her. The more a lovely secret was real the less you spoke of it. But as the secret came to evanesce, as soon as it threatened to go away on its own accord, the secret itself grew frantic and indiscreet—as a way to hang on to its own fading life.

Now they had gotten lucky at long last and neither of them was married anymore—though anything that was at long last, and that had involved such miserable commotion, was unlikely to be truly lucky. They had arranged this rendezvous in faraway France, and neither of them knew its meaning, for its meaning had not been determined out loud. "Is this a date, or independent contractors in semi-prearranged collision?" he had asked just last night, and then spring rain had poured down upon them, shining the concrete, dripping off both their eyeglasses, which they removed, and she had kissed him.

A private car now pulled up at the curb.

"Good God," he said, "the car came so fast."

"Keep eating. That comes first. Eat whatever you can. The car can wait."

She could see he had no appetite but was force-feeding, pushing the food in as if it were a job. Small bites of the lamb. "People are indeed sheep," he said now, chewing. "Stupid as sheep. Actually with sheep at least one of them is always smart and the others just turn their brains off and follow. 'What's Maurie doing now?' they ask each other. 'Where is Maurie going, let's follow!' The flock is the organism."

"Like the military," she said.

He swallowed with some difficulty and at first did not say anything. "Yeah. Occasionally. Civ-Mil has never worked properly as a unit." He pulled a bay leaf out of his couscous. "Bay leaves are bullshit," he said, flinging it down on his plate.

"What will you do with the rest of your time here?" he asked, rounding up the remaining food with his fork, pushing it into small piles, with rivulets and valleys.

"I'll find things," she said. "But it will not be the same without you."

He put his fork down and grabbed her hand, which put a knot in her chest.

"Remember: never drink alone," he said.

"I don't," she said. "I usually drink with MacNeil-Lehrer." She assumed he would call her when he got to D.C.

He withdrew his hand, fumbled with his wallet, threw cash down on the table, and grabbed his suitcase.

They got up together and walked to his car. The blue-bereted driver got out and opened the door for him. Tom tossed the bag in the back and turned to her, about to say something, then changed his mind and just got in. When the door shut, he lowered his window.

"I don't know how to say this," he said, "but, well—keep me in mind."

"How could I not?" she said.

"That's something I don't ask, ma chère." She lowered her head, and he pressed his lips to her cheek for a very long moment.

"May our paths cross again soon," she said, stepping back. And then like a deaf person she made a little gesture of a cross with the index fingers of each of her hands, but it came out like a werewolf ward-off sign. Inept even at sign language. A Freudian slip of the dumb. As the car began to roll away, she called out, "Have a good flight!" His head turned and bent toward her one last time.

"Hey, I've got all my liquids packed in my unchecked bag," he shouted, not without innuendo. She flung one palm quickly to her mouth to blow a kiss, but the car took a quick right down the Rue du Bac. A kiss blown—in all ways. But she could see him lift his left hand quickly at the window, like a karate chop that was also a salute, as the car merged and disappeared into the fanning traffic.

Years earlier, at a Christmas party of a mutual friend, their spouses both out on the wintry summer porch smoking, she had found herself next to him, in the kitchen, jiggling the open bottles of wine to see which one might not yet be empty. The day before, along with a photo of prizewinning gingerbread houses on display at the mall, he had sent her an e-mail: "I just took three Adderall and made these for you." In the next room Bob Dylan was singing "Gotta Serve Somebody."

"What is the thing you regret most in life?" he asked her, standing close. There were perhaps a dozen empty bottles, and she and Tom methodically tipped every one of them upside down, held them up to the light, sometimes peering into them from underneath. "Nothing but dead soldiers here," he murmured. "I'd like to say optimistically that they were half full, not half empty, but these are just totally empty."

"Unless you have a life of great importance," she said, "regrets are stupid, crumpled-up tickets to a circus that has already left town."

His face went bright with amusement and drink. "Then what happens to the town?" he asked.

She thought about this. "Oh, there's a lot of weather," she said, slowly. "It snows. It thunders. The sun comes out. People go to church and sit in the sanctuary and sometimes they see escaped clowns sitting in the back pews with their white gloves still on."

"Escaped clowns?" he asked.

"Escaped," she said. "Sort of escaped."

"Come in from the cold?" he inquired.

"Come in to sit next to each other."

He nodded with satisfaction. "The past is for losers, baby?"

"Kind of like that." She wasn't sure that she agreed, but she understood the power of such a thought.

His stance grew jaunty. He leaned in close to her, up against the kitchen counter's edge.

"Do you ever feel that no one knows what you're talking about, that everyone is just pretending—except for me?"

She studied him carefully. "Yes, I do," she said. "I do."

"Ah," he replied, straightening his posture. He clasped her hand: electricity burst into it then vanished as he let go. "We're all suckers for a happy ending."

THANK YOU FOR HAVING ME

The day following Michael Jackson's death, I was constructing my own memorial for him. I played his videos on YouTube and sat in the kitchen at night, with the iPod light at the table's center the only source of illumination. I listened to "Man in the Mirror" and "Ben," my favorite, even if it was about a killer rat. I tried not to think about its being about a rat, as it was also the name of an old beau, who had e-mailed me from Istanbul upon hearing of Jackson's death. Apparently there was no one in Turkey to talk about it with. "When I heard the news of MJackson's death I thought of you," the ex-beau had written, "and that sweet, loose-limbed dance you used to do to one of his up-tempo numbers."

I tried to think positively. "Well, at least Whitney Houston didn't die," I said to someone on the phone. Every minute that ticked by in life contained very little information, until suddenly it contained too much.

"Mom, what are you doing?" asked my fifteen-year-old daughter, Nickie. "You look like a crazy lady sitting in the kitchen like this."

"I'm just listening to some music."

"But like this?"

"I didn't want to disturb you."

"You are so totally disturbing me," she said.

Nickie had lately announced a desire to have her own reality show so that the world could see what she had to put up with.

I pulled out the earbuds. "What are you wearing tomorrow?"

"Whatever. I mean, does it matter?"

"Uh, no. Not really." Nickie sauntered out of the room. Of course it did not matter what young people wore: they were already amazing looking, without really knowing it, which was also part of their beauty. I was going to be Nickie's date at the wedding of Maria, her former babysitter, and Nickie was going to be mine. The person who needed to be careful what she wore was me.

It was a wedding in the country, a half-hour drive, and we arrived on time, but somehow we seemed the last ones there. Guests milled about semipurposefully. Maria, an attractive, restless Brazilian, was marrying a local farm boy, for the second time—a second farm boy on a second farm. The previous farm boy she had married, Ian, was present as well. He had been hired to play music, and as the guests floated by with their plastic cups of wine, Ian sat there playing a slow melancholic version of "I Want You Back." Except he didn't seem to want her back. He was smiling and nodding at everyone and seemed happy to be part of this send-off. He was the entertainment. He wore a T-shirt that read, THANK YOU FOR HAVING ME. This seemed remarkably sanguine and useful as well as a little beautiful. I wondered how it was done. I myself had never done anything remotely similar. "Marriage is one long conversation," wrote Robert Louis Stevenson. Of course, he died when he was forty-four, so he had no idea how long the conversation could really get to be.

"I can't believe you wore that," Nickie whispered to me in her mauve eyelet sundress.

"I know. It probably was a mistake." I was wearing a synthetic leopard-print sheath: I admired camouflage. A leopard's markings I'd imagined existed because a leopard's habitat had once been alive with snakes, and blending in was required. Leopards were frightened of snakes and also of chimpanzees, who were in turn frightened of leopards—a standoff between predator and prey, since there was a confusion as to which was which: this was also a theme in the wilds of my closet. Perhaps I had watched too many nature documentaries.

"Maybe you could get Ian some lemonade," I said to Nickie. I had already grabbed some wine from a passing black plastic tray.

"Yes, maybe I could," she said and loped across the yard. I watched her broad tan back and her confident gait. She was a gorgeous giantess. I was in awe to have such a daughter. Also in fear—as in fearful for my life.

"It's good you and Maria have stayed friends," I said to Ian. Ian's father, who had one of those embarrassing father-in-law crushes on his son's departing wife, was not taking it so well. One could see him misty-eyed, treading the edge of the property with some iced gin, keeping his eye out for Maria, waiting for her to come out of the house, waiting for an opening, when she might be free of others, so he could rush up and embrace her.

"Yes." Ian smiled. Ian sighed. And for a fleeting moment everything felt completely fucked up.

And then everything righted itself again. It felt important spiritually to go to weddings: to give balance to the wakes and memorial services. People shouldn't have been set in motion on this planet only to grieve losses. And without weddings there were only funerals. I had seen a soccer mom become a rhododendron with a plaque, next to the soccer field parking lot, as if it had been watching all those matches that had killed her. I had seen a brilliant young student become a creative writing contest, as if it were all that writing that had been the thing to do him in. And I had seen a public defender become a justice fund, as if one paid for fairness with one's very life. I had seen a dozen people become hunks of rock with their names engraved so shockingly perfectly upon the surface it looked as if they had indeed turned to stone, been given a new life the way the moon is given it, through some lighting tricks and a face-like font. I had turned a hundred Rolodex cards around to their blank sides. So let a babysitter become a bride again. Let her marry over and over. So much urgent and lifelike love went rumbling around underground and died there, never got expressed at all, so let some errant inconvenient attraction have its way. There was so little time.

Someone very swanky and tall and in muddy high heels in the grass was now standing in front of Ian, holding a microphone, and singing "Waters of March" while Ian accompanied. My mind imitated the song by wandering: A stick. A stone. A wad of cow pie. A teary mom's eye.

"There are a bazillion Brazilians here," said Nickie, arriving with two lemonades.

"What did you expect?" I took one of the lemonades for Ian and put my arm around her.

"I don't know. I only ever met her sister. Just once. The upside is at least I'm not the only one wearing a color."

We gazed across the long yard of the farmhouse. Maria's sister and her mother were by the rosebushes, having their pictures taken without the bride.

"Maria and her sister both look like their mother." Her mother and I had met once before, and I now nodded in her direction across the yard. I couldn't tell if she could see me.

Nickie nodded with a slight smirk. "Their father died in a car crash. So yeah, they don't look like him."

I swatted her arm. "Nickie. Sheesh."

She was silent for a while. "Do you ever think of Dad?"

"Dad who?"

"Come on."

"You mean, Dad-eeeeee?"

The weekend her father left—left the house, the town, the country, everything, packing so lightly I believed he would come back—he had said, "You can raise Nickie by yourself. You'll be good at it."

And I had said, "Are you on crack?" And he had replied, continuing to fold a blue twill jacket, "Yes, a little."

"Dadder. As in *badder*," Nickie said now. She sometimes claimed to friends that her father had died, and when she was asked how, she would gaze bereavedly off into the distance and say, "A really, really serious game of Hangman." Mothers and their only children of divorce were a skewed family dynamic, if they were families at all. Perhaps they were more like cruddy buddy movies, and the dialogue between them was unrecognizable as filial or parental. It was extraterrestrial. With a streak of dog-walkers-meeting-at-the-park. It contained more sibling banter than it should have. Still, I preferred the whole thing to being a lonely old spinster, the fate I once thought I was most genetically destined for, though I'd worked hard, too hard, to defy and avoid it, when perhaps there it lay ahead of me regardless. If you were alone when you were born, alone when you were dying, *really absolutely* alone when you were dead, why "learn to be alone" in between? If you had forgotten, it would quickly come back to you. Aloneness was like riding a bike. At gunpoint. With the gun in your own hand. Aloneness was the air in your tires, the wind in your hair. You didn't have to go looking for it with open arms. With open arms, you fell off the bike: I was drinking my wine too quickly.

Maria came out of the house in her beautiful shoulderless wedding dress, which was white as could be.

"What a fantastic costume," said Nickie archly.

Nickie was both keen observer and enthusiastic participant in the sartorial disguise department, and when she was little there had been much playing of Wedding, fake bridal bouquets made of ragged plastic-handled sponges tossed up into the air and often into the garage basketball hoop, catching there. She was also into Halloween. She would trick-or-treat for UNICEF dressed in a sniper outfit or a suicide bomber outfit replete with vest. Once when she was eight, she went as a dryad, a tree nymph, and when asked at doors what she was, she kept saying, "A tree-nip." She had been a haughty trick-or-treater, alert to the failed adult guessing game of it—*you're a what? a vampire?*—so when the neighbors looked confused, she scowled and said reproachfully, "Have you *never* studied Greek mythology?" Nickie knew how to terrify. She had sometimes been more interested in answering our own door than in knocking on others, peering around the edge of it with a witch hat and a loud cackle. "I think it's time to get back to the customers," she announced to me one Halloween when she was five, grabbing my hand and racing back to our house. She was fearless: she had always chosen the peanut allergy table at school since a boy she liked sat there—the cafeteria version of *The Magic Mountain*. Nickie's childhood, like all dreams, sharpened artificially into stray vignettes when I tried to conjure it, then faded away entirely. Now tall and long-limbed and inscrutable, she seemed more than ever like a sniper. I felt paralyzed beside her, and the love I had for her was less for this new spiky Nickie than for the old spiky one, which was still inside her somewhere, though it was a matter of faith to think so. Surely that was why faith had been invented: to raise teenagers without dying. Although of course it was also why death was invented: to escape teenagers altogether. When, in the last few months, Nickie had "stood her ground" in various rooms of the house, screaming at me abusively, I would begin mutely to disrobe, slowly lifting my shirt over my head so as not to see her, and only that would send her flying out of the room in disgust. Only nakedness was silencing, but at least something was.

"I can't believe Maria's wearing white," said Nickie.

I shrugged. "What color should she wear?"

"Gray!" Nickie said immediately. "To acknowledge having a brain! A little gray matter!"

"Actually, I saw something on PBS recently that said only the outer bark of the brain—and it does look like bark—is gray. Apparently the other half of the brain has a lot of white matter. For connectivity."

Nickie snorted, as she often did when I uttered the letters *PBS*. "Then she should wear gray in acknowledgment of having half a brain."

I nodded. "I get your point," I said.

Guests were eating canapés on paper plates and having their pictures taken with the bride. Not so much with Maria's new groom, a boy named Hank, which was short not for Henry but for Johannes, and who was not wearing sunglasses like everyone else but was sort of squinting at Maria in pride and disbelief. Hank was also a musician, though he mostly repaired banjos and guitars, restrung and varnished them, and that was how he, Maria, and Ian had all met.

Now the air was filled with the old-silver-jewelry smell of oncoming rain. I edged toward Ian, who was looking for the next song, idly strumming, trying not to watch his father eye Maria.

"Whatcha got? 'I'll Be There'?" I asked cheerfully. I had always liked Ian. He had chosen Maria like a character, met her on a semester abroad and then come home already married to her—much to the marveling of his dad. Ian loved Maria, and was always loyal to her, no matter what story she was in, but Maria was a narrative girl and the story had to be spellbinding or she lost interest in the main character, who was sometimes herself and sometimes not. She was destined to marry and marry and marry. Ian smiled and began to sing "I Will Always Love You," sounding oddly like Bob Dylan but without the sneer.

I swayed. I stayed. I did not get in the way.

"You are a saint," I said when he finished. He was a sweet boy, and when Nickie was little he had often come over and played soccer in the yard with her and Maria.

"Oh no, I'm just a deposed king of corn. She bought the farm. I mean, I sold it to her, and then she flipped it and bought this one instead." He motioned toward the endless field beyond the tent, where the corn was midget and standing in mud, June not having been hot enough to evaporate the puddles. The tomatoes and marijuana would not do well this year. "Last night I had a dream that I was in *West Side Story* and had forgotten all the words to 'I like to be in America.' Doesn't take a genius to figure that one out."

"No," I said. "I guess not."

"Jesus, what is my dad *doing*?" Ian said, looking down and away.

Ian's father was still prowling the perimeter, a little drunkenly, not taking his eyes off the bride.

"The older generation," I said, shaking my head, as if it didn't include me. "They can't take any change. There's too much missingness that has already accumulated. They can't take any more."

"Geez," Ian said, glancing up and over again. "I wish my dad would just get over her."

I swallowed more wine while holding Ian's lemonade. Over by the apple tree there were three squirrels. A threesome of squirrels looked ominous, like a plague. "What other songs ya got?" I asked him. Nickie was off talking to Johannes Hank.

"I have to save a couple for the actual ceremony."

"There's going to be an actual ceremony?"

"Sort of. Maybe not *actual* actual. They have things they want to recite to each other."

"Oh yes, that," I said.

"They're going to walk up together from this canopy toward the house, say whatever, and then people get to eat." Everyone had brought food, and it was spread out on a long table between the house and the barn. I had brought two large roaster chickens, cooked accidentally on Clean while I was listening to Michael Jackson on my iPod. But the chickens had looked OK,

I thought: hanging off the bone a bit but otherwise fine, even
if not as fine as when they had started and had been Amish and
air-chilled and a fortune. When I had bought them the day
before at Whole Foods and gasped at the total on my receipt,
the cashier had said, "Yes. Some people know how to shop here
and some people don't."

"Thirty-three thirty-three. Perhaps that's good luck."

"Yup. It's about as lucky as two dead birds get to be," said
the cashier.

"Is there a priest or anything? Will the marriage be legal?" I
now asked Ian.

Ian smiled and shrugged.

"They're going to say 'You do' after the other one says 'I do.'
Double indemnity."

I put his lemonade down on a nearby table and gave him a
soft chuck on the shoulder. We both looked across the yard at
Hank, who was wearing a tie made of small yellow pop beads
that formed themselves into the shape of an ear of corn. It had
ingeniousness and tackiness both, like so much else created by
people.

"That's a lot of *do*s."

"I know. But I'm not making a beeline for the jokes."

"The jokes?"

"The doozy one, the do-do one. I'm not going to make any
of them."

"Why would you make jokes? It's not like you're the best
man."

Ian looked down and twisted his mouth a little.

"Oh, dear. You *are*?" I said. I squinted at him. When young
I had practiced doing the upside-down wink of a bird.

"Don't ask," he said.

"Hey, look." I put my arm around him. "George Harrison did it. And no one thought twice. Or, well, no one thought more than twice."

Nickie approached me quickly from across the grass. "Mom. Your chickens look disgusting. It's like they were hit by a truck."

The wedding party had started to line up—except Ian, who had to play. They were going to get this ceremony over with quickly, before the storm clouds to the west drifted near and made things worse. The bridesmaids began stepping first, a short trajectory from the canopy to the rosebushes, where the *I do*s would be said. Ian played "Here Comes the Bride." The bridesmaids were in pastels: one the light peach of baby aspirin; one the seafoam green of low-dose clonazepam; the other the pale daffodil of the next lowest dose of clonazepam. What a good idea to have the look of Big Pharma at your wedding. Why hadn't I thought of that? Why hadn't I thought of that until now?

"I take thee, dear Maria . . ." They were uttering these promises themselves just as Ian said they would. Hank said, "I do," and Maria said, "You do." Then vice versa. At least Maria had taken off her sunglasses. *Young people,* I tried not to say out loud with a sigh. Time went slowly, then stood still, then became undetectable, so who knew how long all this was taking?

A loud noise like mechanized thunder was coming from the highway. Strangely, it was not a storm. A group of motorcyclists boomed up the road and, instead of roaring by us, slowed, then turned right in at the driveway, a dozen of them—all on Harleys. I didn't really know motorcycles, but I knew that every biker from Platteville to Manitowoc owned a Harley. That was just a regional fact. They switched off their engines. None of the riders wore a helmet—they wore bandannas—except for the leader, who wore a football helmet with some plush puppy ears which had been snipped from some child's stuffed animal then glued on either side. He took out a handgun and fired it three times into the air.

Several guests screamed. I could make no sound at all.

The biker with the gun and the puppy ears began to shout. "I have a firearms license and those were blanks and this is self-defense because our group here has an easement that extends just this far into this driveway. Also? We were abused as children and as adults and moreover we have been eating a hell of a lot of Twinkies. Also? We are actually very peaceful people. We just know that life can get quite startling in its switches of channels. That there is a river and sea figure of speech as well as a TV one. Which is why as life moves rudely past, you have to give it room. We understand that. An occasion like this means No More Forks in the Road. All mistakes are behind you, and that means it's no longer really possible to make one. Not a big one. You already done that. I need to speak first here to the bride." He looked around, but no one moved. He cleared his throat a bit. "The errors a person already made can step forward and announce themselves and then freeze themselves into a charming little sculpture garden that can no longer hurt you. Like a cemetery. And like a cemetery it is the kind of freedom that is the opposite of free." He looked in a puzzled way across the property toward Maria. "It's the flickering quantum zone of gun and none, got and not." He shifted uncomfortably, as if the phrase "flickering quantum zone" had taken a lot out of him. "As I said, now I need to speak to the bride. Would that be you?"

Maria shouted at him in Portuguese. Her bridesmaids joined in.

"What are they saying?" I murmured to Nickie.

"I forgot all my Portuguese," she said. "My whole childhood I only remember Maria saying 'good job' to everything I did, so I now think of that as Portuguese."

"Yes," I murmured. "So do I."

"Good job!" Nickie shouted belligerently at the biker. "Good job being an asshole and interrupting a wedding!"

"Nickie, leave this to the grown-ups," I whispered.

But the guests just stood there, paralyzed, except Ian, who, seemingly very far off on the horizon, slowly stood, placing his guitar on the ground. He then took his white collapsible chair in both hands and raised it over his head.

"Are you Caitlin?" The puppy-eared biker continued to address Maria, and she continued to curse, waving her sprigs of mint and spirea at him. *"Và embora, babaca!"* She gave him the finger, and when Hank tried to calm her, she gave Hank the finger. *"Fodase!"*

The cyclist looked around with an expression that suggested he believed he might have the wrong country wedding. He took out his cell phone, took off his helmet, pressed someone on speed dial, then turned to speak into it. "Yo! Joe. I don't think you gave me the right address . . . yeah . . . no, you don't get it. This ain't Caitlin's place. . . . What? No, listen! What I'm saying is: wrong addressee! This ain't it. No speaky zee English here—" He slammed his phone shut. He put his helmet back on. But Ian was trotting slowly toward him with the chair over his head, crying the yelping cry of anyone who was trying to be a hero at his ex-wife's wedding.

"Sorry, people," the biker said. He gave the approaching Ian only a quick unfazed double-take. He flicked one of his puppy ears at him and hurried to straddle his bike. "Wrong address, everybody!" Then his whole too-stoned-to be-menacing gang started up their engines and rode away in a roar, kicking up dust from the driveway gravel. It was a relief to see them go. Ian continued to run down the road after them, howling, chair overhead, though the motorcycles were quickly out of sight.

"Should we follow Ian?" asked Nickie. Someone near us was phoning the police.

"Let Ian get it out of his system," I said.

"Yeah," she said and now made a beeline for Maria.

"Good job!" I could hear Nickie say to Maria. "Good job getting married!" And then Nickie threw her arms around her former caretaker and began, hunched and heaving, to weep on her shoulder. I couldn't bear to watch. There was a big black zigzag across my heart. I could hear Maria say, "Tank you for combing, Nickie. You and your muzzer are my hairos."

Ian had not returned and no one had gone looking for him. He would be back in time for the rain. There was a rent-a-disc-jockey who started to put on some music, which blared from the speakers. Michael Jackson again. Every day there was something new to mourn and something old to celebrate: civilization had learned this long ago and continued to remind us. Was that what the biker had meant? I moved toward the buffet table.

"You know, when you're hungry, there's nothing better than food," I said to a perfect stranger. I cut a small chunk of ham.

I place a deviled egg in my mouth and resisted the temptation to position it in front of my teeth and smile scarily, the way we had as children. I chewed and swallowed and grabbed another one. Soon no doubt I would resemble a large vertical snake who had swallowed a rat. That rat Ben. Snakes would eat a sirloin steak only if it was disguised behind the head of a small rodent. There was a lesson somewhere in there and just a little more wine would reveal it.

"Oh, look at those sad chickens!" I said ambiguously and with my mouth full. There were rumors that the wedding cake was still being frosted and that it would take a while. A few people were starting to dance, before the dark clouds burst open and ruined everything. Next to the food table was a smaller one displaying a variety of insect repellents, aerosols and creams, as if it were the vanity corner of a posh ladies' room, except with discrete constellations of gnats. Guests were spraying themselves a little too close to the food, and the smells of citronella and imminent rain combined in the air.

The biker was right: you had to unfreeze your feet, take blind steps backward, risk a loss of balance, risk an endless fall, in order to give life room. Was that what he had said? Who knew? People were shaking their bodies to Michael Jackson's "Shake Your Body." I wanted this song played at my funeral. Also the Doobie Brothers' "Takin' It to the Streets." Also "Have Yourself a Merry Little Christmas"—just to fuck with people.

I put down my paper plate and plastic wineglass. I looked over at Ian's dad, who was once again brooding off by himself. "Come dance with someone your own age!" I called to him, and because he did not say, "That is so not going to happen," I approached him from across the lawn. As I got closer I could see that since the days he would sometimes come to our house to pick up Maria and drive her home himself in the silver sports car of the recently single, he had had some eye work done: a lift to remove the puff and bloat; he would rather look startled and insane than look fifty-six. I grabbed both his hands and reeled him around. "Whoa," he said with something like a smile, and he let go with one hand to raise it over his head and flutter it in a jokey jazz razzamatazz. In sign language it was the sign for applause. I needed my breath for dancing, so I tried not to laugh. Instead I fixed my face into a grin, and, ah, for a second the sun came out to light up the side of the red and spinning barn.

Acknowledgments

For their generous reading and helpful insights, thank you to Julian Barnes, Charles Baxter, Melanie Jackson, Mona Simpson, Lorin Stein, and Victoria Wilson.